GLIMMER TRAIN
STORIES

EDITORS
Susan Burmeister-Brown
Linda Burmeister Davies

CONSULTING EDITORS
Dave Chipps
Britney Gress
Tamara Moan

COPY EDITOR & PROOFREADER
Scott Allie

TYPESETTING & LAYOUT
Heidi Weitz Siegel

COVER ILLUSTRATOR
Jane Zwinger

STORY ILLUSTRATOR
Jon Leon

PUBLISHED QUARTERLY
in spring, summer, fall, and winter by
Glimmer Train Press, Inc.
710 SW Madison Street, Suite 504
Portland, Oregon 97205-2900 U.S.A.
Telephone: 503/221-0836
Facsimile: 503/221-0837
www.glimmertrain.com

PRINTED IN U.S.A.
Indexed in *The American Humanities Index.*

Glimmer Train (ISSN #1055-7520), registered in U.S. Patent and Trademark Office, is published quarterly, $32 per year in the U.S., by Glimmer Train Press, Inc., Suite 504, 710 SW Madison, Portland, OR 97205. Second-class postage paid at Portland, OR, and additional mailing offices. POSTMASTER: Send address changes to Glimmer Train Press, Inc., Suite 504, 710 SW Madison, Portland, OR 97205.

STATEMENT OF OWNERSHIP, MANAGEMENT, AND CIRCULATION. Required by 39 USC 3685, anticipated file date: 10/97. Publication name: Glimmer Train, publication #10557520. Published quarterly (4x/yr). Publisher and owner: Glimmer Train Press, Inc. Complete mailing address of known office of publication and headquarters is 710 SW Madison, #504, Portland, OR 97205-2900. Editors and co-presidents: Susan Burmeister-Brown and Linda Burmeister Davies, 710 SW Madison, #504, Portland, OR 97205-2900. Known bondholders: none. Extent and nature of circulation: a) average number of copies each issue during preceding 12 months, b) actual number of copies of single issue published nearest to filing date. Net press run: a) eleven thousand, three hundred twenty-five; b) thirteen thousand. Distributor sales: a) one thousand, five hundred ninety-eight; b) one thousand, six hundred eleven. Paid or requested mailed subscriptions: a) five thousand, seven hundred one; b) seven thousand, two hundred twenty-seven. Total paid/requested circulation: a) seven thousand, two hundred ninety-nine; b) eight thousand, eight hundred thirty-eight. Free distribution by mail: a) one hundred; b) one hundred. Free distribution outside of mail: a) one hundred five; b) one hundred five. Total free distribution: a) two hundred five; b) two hundred five. Total distribution: a) seven thousand, five hundred four; b) nine thousand forty-three. Copies not distributed: a) one thousand, eight hundred sixty-seven; b) one thousand, nine hundred eighty-eight. Copies returned from news agents: a) one thousand, nine hundred fifty-four; b) one thousand nine hundred sixty-nine. Total sum of distributed and not distributed copies: a) eleven thousand, three hundred twenty-five; b) thirteen thousand. I certify that the statements made by me above are correct and complete—Linda Burmeister Davies, Editor.

ISSN # 1055-7520, ISBN # 1-880966-24-7, CPDA BIPAD # 79021

DISTRIBUTION: Bookstores can purchase *Glimmer Train Stories* through these distributors:
Anderson News Co., 6016 Brookvale Ln., #151, Knoxville, TN 37919
Ingram Periodicals, 1226 Heil Quaker Blvd., LaVergne, TN 37086
IPD, 674 Via de la Valle, #204, Solana Beach, CA 92075
Peribo PTY Ltd., 58 Beaumont Rd., Mt. Kuring-Gai, NSW 2080, AUSTRALIA
Ubiquity, 607 Degraw St., Brooklyn, NY 11217

SUBSCRIPTION SVCS: EBSCO, Faxon, READMORE

Subscription rates: One year, $32 within the U.S. (Visa/MC/check). Airmail to Canada, $43; outside North America, $54. Payable by Visa/MC or check for U.S. dollars drawn on a U.S. bank.

Attention short-story writers: *We pay $500 for first publication and onetime anthology rights. Please include a self-addressed, sufficiently stamped envelope with your submission.* **Send manuscripts in January, April, July, and October.** *Send a SASE for guidelines, which will include information on our Short-Story Award for New Writers.*

$\mathcal{D}$edication

Our twenty-fifth issue
we dedicate to our wonderful mom,
Dorothy Grace Burmeister,
who died on July 28, 1970, of brain cancer.

Thank you for still looking after us.

Linda & Susan

CONTENTS

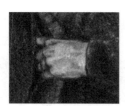

$\mathscr{C}$ONTENTS

Monica Wood

Here I am at 16 Worthley Avenue in Mexico, Maine.
I'm on the left, my sister Betty is on the right, and the cutie
in the middle is my big sister, Anne. My youngest sister, Cathe,
is tucked into a crib in our third-floor apartment, and my brother,
Barry, is overseas in the army. One result of the age span in my
family is that Anne became my high-school English teacher,
an event that cemented my interest in writing. And as you
can probably tell from this photo, I grew up feeling adored.

Monica Wood is the author of *Secret Language*, a novel; *Description*, a fiction-writers' manual; and two guides to contemporary literature for the high-school classroom. Her short stories have appeared in *Glimmer Train*, *Manoa*, *North American Review*, *Redbook*, *Yankee*, *Tampa Review*, and many other magazines and anthologies. She lives in Portland, Maine, where she is on the home stretch of her second novel, tentatively titled *My Only Story*.

monica Wood

MONICA WOOD
Ernie's Ark

*E*rnie was an angry man. He felt his anger as something apart from him, like an urn of water balanced on his head, a precarious weight that affected his gait, the set of his shoulders, his willingness to move through a crowd. He was angry at the melon-faced CEO from New York City who had closed a paper mill all the way up in Maine—a decision made, Ernie was sure, in that fancy restaurant atop the World Trade Center where Ernie had taken his wife, Marie, for their forty-second wedding anniversary last May, another season, another life. Every Thursday as he stood in line at Manpower Services to wait for his unemployment check he thought of that jelly-assed CEO whose name he could never manage— McKay or McCoy or some such—yucking it up at a table decked to the nines in bleached linen and phony silver, figuring out all the ways he could cut a man off at the knees two years before retirement.

Oh, yes, he was angry. At the deadbeats and no-accounts who stood in line with him, the Davis boy who couldn't look a man in the eye, the Shelton girl with hair dyed so bright you could light a match on her ponytail. There were others in line—pipefitters and tinsmiths and machine tenders booted out of the mill like diseased dogs—but he couldn't bear to look

Glimmer Train Stories, Issue 25, Winter 1998
©*1997 Monica Wood*

at them, so he reserved his livid stare for the people in line who least resembled himself.

And he was angry at the kids from Broad Street who cut through his yard on their dirt bikes day after day, leaving moats of mud through the flowery back lawn Marie had sprinkled a season ago with Meadow-in-a-Can. And he was angry with the police department, who didn't give a hoot about Marie's wrecked grass. He'd even tried City Hall, where an overpaid blowhard, whose uncle had worked beside Ernie for ten years on the Number Five, had all but laughed in his face.

When he arrived at the hospital after collecting his weekly check, Marie was being bathed by a teenaged orderly. He had seen his wife in all manner of undress during their forty-two years together, yet it filled him with shame to see the yellow hospital sponge applied to her diminishing body by a uniformed kid who was younger than their youngest grandchild. He went to the lobby to wait, picking up a newspaper from among the litter of magazines.

It was some sort of college paper, filled with mean political comics and smug picture captions fashioned to embarrass the President, but it had a separate section on the arts, Marie's favorite subject. She had dozens of coffee-table books stowed in her sewing room, and their house was filled with framed prints of strange objects—melted watches and spent shoelaces and sad, deserted diners—that he never liked but had nonetheless come to think of as old friends. In forty-two years he had never known her to miss a Community Concert or an exhibit at the library, and every Sunday of their married life Ernie had brought in the paper, laid it on the kitchen table, and fished out the arts section to put next to Marie's coffee cup.

The college paper was printed on dirty newsprint—paper from out of state, he surmised. He scanned the cheap, see-through pages, fixing on an announcement for an installation competition, whatever that was. The winning entry would be displayed to the public at the university. Pictured was last year's winner, a tangle of pipes and sheet metal that looked as if somebody had hauled a miniature version of the Number Five machine out of the mill, twisted it into a thousand ugly pieces, then left it to weather through five hundred hailstorms. Not that it would matter now if somebody did. *The Burden of Life*, this installation was called, by an artist who most likely hadn't yet moved out of his parents' house. He thought Marie would like it, though—she had always been a woman who understood people's intentions—so he removed the picture with his jackknife and tucked it into his shirt pocket and faltered his way back up the hall and into her room, where she was sitting up, weak and clean.

"Can you feature this?" he asked, showing her the clipping. She smiled. "*The Burden of Life?*"

"He should've called it *The Burden of My Big Head.*"

She laughed, and he was glad, and his day took the tiniest turn. "Philistine," she said. "You always were such a philistine, Ernie." She often referred to him in the past tense, as if he were the one departing.

That night he hung the clipping on the refrigerator before taking Pumpkin Pie, Marie's dottering Yorkshire terrier, for its evening walk. He often waited until nightfall for this walk, so mortified was he to drag this silly-named pushbroom of an animal at the end of a thin red leash. The dog walked with prissy little steps on pinkish feet that resembled ballerina slippers. He had observed so many men just like himself over the years, men in retirement walking wee, quivery dogs over the streets of their neighborhood, a wrinkled plastic bag in their free hand; they might as well have been holding a sign above their heads: Widower.

The night was eerie and silent, this end of town strangely naked without the belching smokestacks of Atlantic Pulp & Paper curling up from the valley, an upward, omnipresent cloud rising like a smoke signal, an offering to God. Cancer City, a news reporter once called this place, but gone now was the steam, the smoke, the rising cloud, the heaps and heaps of wood stacked in the railyard, even the smell—the smell of money, Ernie called it—all gone. Every few weeks there was word of negotiation—another fancy-restaurant meeting between McCoy's boys and Atlantic's alleged union—but Ernie held little hope of recovering the bulk of his pension. *For Sale* signs were popping up even in this neighborhood of old people. The city, once drenched with ordinary hopes and good money, was beginning to furl like an autumn leaf.

As he turned up his walk he caught the kids from Broad Street crashing again through his property, this time roaring away so fast he could hear a faint shudder from the backyard trees. "Sonsabitches!" he hollered, shaking his fist like the mean old man in the movies. He stampeded into the backyard, where Marie's two apple trees, brittle and untrained, sprouted from the earth in such rootlike twists that they seemed to have been planted upside down. He scanned the weedy lawn, dotted with hopeful clumps of Marie's wildflowers and the first of the fallen leaves, and saw blowdown everywhere, spindly parts of branches scattered like bodies on a battlefield. Planted when their son was born, the trees had never yielded a single decent apple, and now they were being systematically mutilated by a pack of ill-bred boys. He picked up a branch and a few sticks, and by the time he reached his kitchen he was weeping, pounding his fist on the table, cursing a God who would let a woman like Marie, a big-boned girl who was sweetness itself, wither beneath the death-white sheets of Maine Medical, twelve long miles from home.

He sat in the kitchen deep into evening. The dog curled up on Marie's chair and snored. He remembered Marie's laughter from the afternoon and tried to harness it, hear it anew, make it last. The sticks lay sprawled and messy on the table in front

10

of him, their leaves stalled halfway between greenery and dust. All of a sudden—and, oh, it was sweet!—Ernie had an artistic inspiration. He stood up with the shock of it, for he was not an artistic man. The sticks, put together at just the right angle, resembled the hull of a boat. He turned them one way, then another, admiring his idea, wishing Marie were here to witness it.

Snapping on the floodlights, he jaunted into the backyard to collect the remaining sticks, hauling them into the house a bouquet at a time. He took the clipping down from the fridge and studied the photograph, trying to get a sense of scale and size. Gathering the sticks, he descended the stairs to the cellar, where he spent most of the night twining sticks and branches with electrical wire. The dog sat at attention, its wet eyes fixed on Ernie's work. By morning the installation was finished. It was the most beautiful thing Ernie had ever seen.

The university was only four blocks from the hospital, but Ernie had trouble navigating the maze of one-way roads on campus, and found the art department only by following the directions of a frightening girl whose tender lips had been pierced with small gold rings. By the time he entered the office of the university art department, he was sweating, hugging his beautiful boat to his chest.

"Excuse me?" said a young man at the desk. This one had a ring through each eyebrow.

"My installation," Ernie said, placing it on the desk. "For the competition." He presented the newspaper clipping like an admission ticket.

"Uh, I don't think so."

"Am I early?" Ernie asked, feeling foolish. The deadline was six weeks away; he hadn't the foggiest idea how these things were supposed to go.

"This isn't an installation," the boy said, flickering his gaze over the boat. "It's—well, I don't know what it is, but it's not an installation."

"It's a boat," Ernie said. "A boat filled with leaves."

"Are you in Elderhostel?" the boy asked. "They're upstairs, fifth floor."

"I want to enter the contest," Ernie said. And by God, he did; he had never won so much as a cake raffle in his life, and didn't like one bit the pileup of things he appeared to be losing.

"I like your boat," said a girl stacking books in a corner. "But he's right, it's not an installation." She spread her arms and smiled. "Installations are big."

Ernie turned to face her, a freckled redhead. She reminded him of his granddaughter, who was somewhere in Oregon sharing her medicine cabinet with an unemployed piano player. "Let me see," the girl said, plucking the clipping from his hand. "Oh, okay. You're talking about the Corthell Competition. This is more of a professional thing."

"Professional?"

"I myself wouldn't *dream* of entering, okay?" offered the boy, who rocked backed in his chair, arms folded like a CEO's. "All the entries come through this office, and most of them are awesome. Museum quality." He made a small, self-congratulating gesture with his hand. "We see the entries even before the judges do."

"One of my professors won last year," the girl said, pointing out the window. "See?"

Ernie looked. There it was, huge in real life—nearly as big as the actual Number Five, in fact, a heap of junk flung without a thought into the middle of a campus lawn. It did indeed look like a Burden.

"You couldn't tell from the picture," Ernie said, reddening. "In the picture it looked like some sort of tabletop size. Something you might put on top of your TV."

The girl smiled. Ernie could gather her whole face without stumbling over a single gold hoop. He took this as a good sign, and asked, "Let's say I did make something of size. How would I get it over here? Do you do pickups, something of that nature?"

She laughed, but not unkindly. "You don't actually build it unless you win. What you do is write up a proposal with some sketches. Then, if you win, you build it right here, on site." She shrugged. "The *process* is the whole entire idea of the installation, okay? The whole entire community learns from witnessing the *process*."

In this office, where "process" was clearly the most important word in the English language, not counting "okay," Ernie felt suddenly small. "Is that so," he said, wondering who learned what from the heap of tin Professor Life-Burden had processed onto the lawn.

"Oh, wait, one year a guy *did* build off site," said the boy, ever eager to correct the world's misperceptions. "Remember that guy?"

"Yeah," the girl said. She turned to Ernie brightly. "One year a guy put his whole installation together at his studio and sent photographs. He didn't win, but the winner got pneumonia or something and couldn't follow through, and this guy was runner-up, so he trucked it here in a U-Haul."

"It was a totem," the boy said solemnly. "With a whole mess of wire things sticking out of it."

"I was a freshman," the girl said by way of an explanation Ernie couldn't begin to fathom. He missed Marie intensely, as if she were already gone.

Ernie peered through the window, hunting for the totem.

"Kappa Delts trashed it last Homecoming," the girl said. "Those animals have no respect for art." She handed back the clipping. "So, anyway, that really wasn't so stupid after all, what you said."

"Well," said the boy, "good luck, okay?"

As Ernie bumbled out the door, the girl called after him,

"It's a nice boat, though. I like it."

At the hospital he set the boat on Marie's window sill, explaining his morning. "Oh, Ernie," Marie crooned. "You old—you old surprise, you."

"They wouldn't take it," he said. "It's not big enough. You have to write the thing up, and make sketches and whatnot."

"So why don't you?"

"Why don't I what?"

"Make sketches and whatnot."

"Hah! I'd make it for real. Nobody does anything real anymore. I'd pack it into the back of my truck and haul it there myself. A guy did that once."

"Then make it for real."

"I don't have enough branches."

"Then use something else."

"I just might."

"Then do it." She was smiling madly now, fully engaged in their old, intimate arguing, and her eyes made bright blue sparks from her papery face. He knew her well, he realized, and saw what she was thinking: Ernie, there is some life left after everything seems to be gone. Really, there is. And that he could see this, just a little, and that she could see him seeing it, buoyed him. He thought he might even detect some pink fading into her cheeks.

He stayed through lunch, and was set to stay for supper until Marie remembered her dog and made him go home. As he turned from her bed, she said, "Wait. I want my ark." She lifted her finger to the window sill, where the boat glistened in the cheesy city light. And he saw that she was right: it *was* an ark, high and round and jammed with hope. He placed it in her arms and left it there, hoping it might sweeten her dreams.

When he reached his driveway he found fresh tire tracks, rutted by an afternoon rain, running in a rude diagonal from the back of the house across the front yard. He sat in the truck for a few minutes, counting the seconds of his rage, watching the dog's jangly shadow in the dining-room window. He counted to two hundred, checked his watch, then hauled himself out to fetch the dog. He set the dog on the seat next to him—in a better life it would have been a Doberman named Rex—and gave it a kiss on its wiry head. "That's from her," he said, and then drove straight to the lumberyard.

Ernie figured that Noah himself was a man of the soil and probably didn't know spit about boatbuilding. In fact, Ernie's experience in general (forty years of tending machinery, fixing industrial pipe the size of tree trunks, assembling Christmas toys for his son and then his grandchildren, remodeling bathrooms, and building bird boxes and planters and a sunporch to please Marie) probably had Noah's beat in about a dozen ways. He figured he had the will and enough good tools to make a stab at a decent ark, and in a week's time had most of a hull completed beneath a makeshift staging. It was not a hull he would care to float, but he thought of it as a decent artistic representation of a hull; and even more important, it was big enough to qualify as an installation, if he had the guidelines right. He covered the hull with the bargain-priced tongue-and-groove boards he picked up at the lumberyard, fourteen footers left over from people who'd wanted eights. He worked from sunup to noon, then drove to the hospital to give Marie a progress report. Often he turned on the floodlights in the evenings and worked till midnight or one. Working in the open air, without the iron skull of the mill over his head, made him feel like a newly sprung prisoner. He let the dog patter around and around the growing apparition, and sometimes he even chuckled at the animal's apparent capacity for wonder. The hateful boys from Broad Street loitered with their bikes at the back of the yard, and as the thing grew in size they more often than not opted for the long way 'round.

At eleven o'clock on the second day of the second week, a middle-aged man pulled up in a city car. He ambled down the walk and along the side yard, a clipboard and notebook clutched under one arm. The dog cowered at the base of one of the trees, its dime-sized eyes blackened with fear.

"You Mr. Ernest Whitten?" the man asked Ernie.

Ernie put down his hammer and climbed down from the deck by way of a gangplank that he had constructed in a late-night fit of creativity.

"I'm Dan Little, from the city," the man said, extending his hand.

"Well," Ernie said, astonished. He pumped the man's hand. "It's about time." He looked at the bike tracks, which had healed over for the most part, dried into faint, innocent-looking scars from two weeks of fine weather. "Not that it matters now," Ernie said. "They don't even come through much anymore."

Mr. Little consulted his notebook. "I don't follow," he said.

"Aren't you here about those hoodlums tearing up my wife's yard?"

"I'm from code enforcement."

"Pardon?"

Mr. Little squinted up at the ark. "You need a building permit for this, Mr. Whitten. Plus the city has a twenty-five-foot setback requirement for any new buildings."

Ernie twisted his face into disbelief, an expression that felt uncomfortably familiar; lately the entire world astonished him. "The lot's only fifty feet wide as it is," he protested.

"I realize that, Mr. Whitten." Mr. Little shrugged apologetically. "I'm afraid you're going to have to take it down."

Ernie tipped back his cap to scratch his head. "It isn't a building. It's an installation."

"Say what?"

"An installation. I'm hauling it up to the college when I'm

done. Figure I'll have to rent a flatbed or something. It's a little bigger than I counted on."

Mr. Little began to look nervous. "I'm sorry, Mr. Whitten, I still don't follow." He kept glancing back at the car.

"It's an ark," Ernie said, enunciating, although he could see how the ark might be mistaken for a building at this stage. Especially if you weren't really looking, which this man clearly wasn't. "It's an ark," Ernie repeated.

Mr. Little's face took a heavy downward turn. "You're not zoned for boatbuilding," he sighed, writing something on the official-pink papers attached to his clipboard.

Ernie glanced at the car. In the driver's seat had appeared a pony-sized yellow Labrador retriever, its quivering nose faced dead forward as if it were planning to set that sucker into gear and take off into the wild blue yonder.

"That your dog?" Ernie asked.

Mr. Little nodded.

"Nice dog," Ernie said.

"This one's yours, I take it?" Mr. Little pointed at Marie's dog, who had scuttled out from the tree and hidden behind Ernie's pants leg.

"My wife's," Ernie told him. "She's in the hospital."

"I'm sorry to hear that," Mr. Little said. "I'm sure she'll be on the mend in no time."

"Doesn't look like it," Ernie said, wondering why he didn't just storm the hospital gates, do something sweeping and biblical, stomp through those clean corridors and defy doctor's orders and pick her up with his bare hands and bring her home.

Mr. Little scooched down and made clicky sounds at Marie's dog, who nosed out from behind Ernie's leg to investigate. "What's his name?" he asked.

"It's, well, it's Pumpkin Pie. My wife named him."

"That's Junie," Mr. Little said, nudging his chin toward the car. "I bought her the day I got divorced, ten years ago. She's a helluva lot more faithful than my wife ever was."

"I never had problems like that," Ernie said.

Mr. Little got to his feet and shook his head at Ernie's ark. "Listen, about this, this—"

"Ark," Ernie said.

"You're going to have do something, Mr. Whitten. At the very least, you'll have to go down to City Hall, get a building permit, and then follow the regulations. Just don't tell them it's a boat. Call it a storage shed or something."

Ernie tipped back his cap again. "I don't suppose it's regulation to cart your dog all over kingdom come on city time."

"Usually she sleeps in the back," Mr. Little said sheepishly.

"I'll tell you what," Ernie said. "You leave my ark alone and I'll keep shut about the dog."

Mr. Little looked sad. "Listen," he said, "people can do what they want as far as I care. But you've got neighbors out here complaining about the floodlights and the noise."

Ernie looked around, half expecting to see the dirt-bike gang sniggering behind their fists someplace out back. But all he saw were *For Sale* signs yellowing from disuse, and the sagging rooftops of his neighbors' houses, their shades drawn against the new, clean-air smell of unemployment.

Mr. Little ripped a sheet off his clipboard and handed it to Ernie. "Look, just consider this a real friendly warning, would you? And just for the record, I hate my job, but I haven't been at it long enough to quit."

Ernie watched him amble back to the car and say something to the dog, who gave her master a walloping with her broad pink tongue. He watched them go, remembering suddenly that he'd seen Mr. Little before, somewhere in the mill—the bleachery maybe, or strolling in the dim recesses near the Number Eight, his face flushed and shiny under his yellow hardhat, clipboard at the ready. Now here he was, harassing senior citizens on behalf of the city. His dog probably provided him with the only scrap of self-respect he could ferret out in a typical day.

Ernie ran a hand over the rough surface of his ark, remembering that Noah's undertaking had been a result of God's despair. God was sorry he'd messed with any of it, the birds of the air and beasts of the forest and especially the two-legged creatures who insisted on lying and cheating and killing their own brothers. Still, God had found one man, one man and his family, worth saving, and therefore had deemed a pair of everything else worth saving, too. "Come on, dog," he said. "We're going to get your mother."

As happened so often, in so many small, miraculous ways in their forty-two years together, Marie had out-thought him. When he got to her room she was fully dressed, her overnight bag perched primly next to her on the bone-white bed, the ark cradled into her lap and tipped on its side. "Ernie," she said, stretching her arms straight out. "Take me home."

He bore her home at twenty-five miles an hour, aware of how every pock in the road rose up to meet her fragile, flesh-wanting spine. He eased her out of the car and carried her over their threshold. He filled all the bird feeders along the sunporch out back, and carried her over to survey the ark. These were her two requests.

By morning she looked better. The weather—the warmest fall on record—held. He propped her on a chaise lounge on the sunporch in the brand-new flannel robe their son's wife had sent from California, then wrapped her in a blanket, so that she looked like a benevolent pod person from a solar system where warmth and decency ruled. The dog nestled in her lap, eyes half-closed in ecstasy.

He propped her there so she could watch him work—her third request. And work he did, feeling the way he had when they were first dating and he would remove his shirt to burrow elaborately into the tangled guts of his forest green 1950 Pontiac. He forgot that he was building the ark for the contest, and how much he wanted to win, and his rage fell like dead leaves from his body as he felt the sunshiney presence of Marie

J. LEON 97-

watching him work. He moved one of Marie's feeders to the deck of the ark because she wanted him to know the tame and chittery company of chickadees. The sun shone and shone; the yard did not succumb to the dun colors of fall; the tracks left by the dirt bikes resembled nothing more ominous than the faintest prints left by dancing birds. Ernie unloaded some more lumber, a stack of roofing shingles, a small door. He had three weeks till deadline, and in this strange, blessed season, he meant to make it.

Marie got better. She sat up, padded around the house a little, ate real food. Several times a day he caught a sharp squeak floating down from the sunporch as she conversed with one of her girlfriends, or with her sister down from Lewiston, or with their son over the phone, or with the visiting nurse. He would look up, see her translucent white hand raised toward him— *It's nothing, Ernie, just go back to whatever you were doing*—and recognize the sound after the fact as a strand of her old laughter, high and ecstatic and small town, like her old self.

"It happens," the nurse told him when he waylaid her on the front walk. "They get a burst of energy toward the end sometimes."

He didn't like this nurse, the way she called Marie "they." He thought of adding her to the list of people and things he'd grown so accustomed to railing against, but because his rage was gone there was no place to put her. He returned to the ark, climbed onto the deck, and began to nail the last shingles to the shallow pitch of the roof. Marie's voice floated out again, and he looked up again, and her hand rose again, and he nodded again, hoping she could see his smiling, his damp collar, the handsome knot of his forearm. He was wearing the clothes he wore to work back when he was working, a grass-colored gabardine shirt and pants—his "greens," Marie called them. In some awful way he recognized this as one of the happiest times of his life; he was brimming with industry and connected to nothing but this one woman, this one patch of earth.

When it was time for Marie's lunch he climbed down from the deck and wiped his hands over his work pants. Mr. Little was standing a few feet away, a camera raised to his face.

"What's this?" Ernie asked.

Mr. Little lowered the camera. "For our records."

Ernie thought on this for a moment. "I'm willing to venture there's nothing like this in your records."

"Not so far," Mr. Little said. He ducked once, twice, as a pair of chickadees flitted over his head. "Your wife is home, I see."

Ernie glanced over at the sunporch, where Marie lay heavily swaddled on her chaise lounge, watching them curiously. He waved at her, and waited many moments as she struggled to free her hand from the blankets and wave back.

"As long as you've got that camera," Ernie said, "I wonder if you wouldn't do us a favor."

"I'm going to have to fine you, Mr. Whitten. I'm sorry."

"I need a picture of my ark," Ernie said. "Would you do us that favor? All you have to do is snap one extra."

Mr. Little looked around uncertainly. "Sure, all right."

"I'm sending it in to a contest."

"I bet you win."

Ernie nodded. "I bet I do."

Mr. Little helped Ernie dismantle the staging, such as it was, and soon the ark stood alone in the sun, as round and full-skirted as a giant hen nestled on the grass. The chickadees, momentarily spooked by the rattle of staging, were back again. Two of them. A pair, Ernie hoped. "Could I borrow your dog?" he asked Mr. Little, whose eyebrows shot up in a question. "Just for a minute," Ernie explained. "For the picture. We get my wife's dog over here and bingo, I got animals two by two. Two birds, two dogs. What else would God need?"

Mr. Little whistled at the city car and out jumped Junie, thundering through the open window, her back end wagging back and forth with her tail. Marie was up now, too, hobbling down the porch stairs, Pumpkin Pie trotting ahead of her, beelining toward Junie's yellow tail. As the dogs sniffed each other, Ernie loped across the grass to help Marie navigate the bumpy spots. "Didn't come to me before now," he told her, "but these dogs are just the ticket." He gentled her over the uneven grass and introduced her to Mr. Little.

"This fellow's donated his dog to the occasion."

Marie held hard to Ernie's arm. She offered her free hand to the pink-tongued Junie and cooed at her. Mr. Little seemed pleased, and didn't hesitate a second when Ernie asked him to lead the dogs up the plank and order them to sit. They did. Then Ernie gathered Marie into his arms—she weighed nothing, his big-boned girl all gone to feathers—and struggled up the plank, next to the dogs. He set Marie on her feet and snugged his arm around her. "Wait till the birds light," he cautioned. Mr. Little waited, then lifted the camera. Everybody smiled.

In the wintry months that followed, Ernie consoled himself with the thought that his ark did not win because he had misunderstood the guidelines, or that he had neglected to name his ark, or that he had no experience putting into words that which could not be put into words. He liked to imagine the panel of judges frowning in confusion over his written material and then halting in awe at the snapshot—holding it up, their faces all riveted at once. He liked especially to imagine the youngsters in the art office, the redheaded girl and the boy with rings, their lives just beginning. Perhaps they felt a brief shudder, a silvery glimpse of the rest of their lives as they removed the snapshot from the envelope. Perhaps they took enough time to see it all—birds lighting on a gunwale, dogs posed on a plank, and a man and woman standing in front of a little door, she in her bathrobe and he in his greens, waiting for rain.

Catherine Seto

Me, at seven, pretending house with my out-of-focus sister.

Catherine Li-Ming Seto is a twenty-four-year-old fiction writer who lives in Ann Arbor, Michigan. She holds an MFA in fiction from the University of Michigan and is currently working on a novel.

CATHERINE SETO

The Other

In the intermission of fall, Indian Summer of '88, Claudia Fong and her parents left their bungalow in the neighborhood of Cabbagetown, where the sound of Toronto streetcars rattled up and down through the side windows of their kitchen. Claudia was given a two-week leave from Longshore High to fly to the coldest place on earth she would ever be, Harbin, tucked high up in the northeast quadrant of China, where the famous Ice Lantern Festivals were held. Her cousin Poy and her aunt, who was rapidly dying and would pass on into the afterworld, were waiting for her—in anticipation: her father had told Poy that Claudia possessed a lucky face, as did his mother.

Claudia Fong had a face that Chinese fortune scholars titled *Two Clear Points, Five Holes Facing Sky*: large lower lobes of ears, rolling forehead, walled nostrils. It was how everything shot high, the way her eyebrows arched, the placement of her brows, the curl at the ends of her lips. She was also born with one breast. What she called "the other," and what most called a congenital void, survived as an inward pucker of skin like a misplaced bellybutton, a quicksand hole that was covered by corrective bras fitted with foam. Her mother made painful efforts to match the corrective bras with what seemed popular with the teenagers, which at Longshore High were ones made of satin and colored brightly in fuschia and royal blue hues.

For years, to abandon any further discussion about reconstructive surgery, her father often told and retold a legend that they, the Fongs, were infamous for sprouting and missing appendages. During the revolt, most of their ancestors were hung by their hair from trees and executed, and the ones that escaped took to the dense bamboo forests of Guandong and eked out their lives as barbarians for the next five generations. After the lengthy duration spent in the forest, her exiled ancestors had supposedly emerged back into civilization with six toes—the sixth appearing just below the pinkie toe, resembling the fleshy nub of an eraser. For provinces all over, it was a mark of honor. The only living relative who bore that symbol was her aunt Yee, and of course, in his opinion, Claudia.

Not once did Claudia feel compelled to accept this explanation, and she would cry in frustration, "So what you're saying is that we come from a long line of proud mutants." Her father would shake his head. "*Lak nouy*, smart girl," he said. "You are too logical for your own good." Maybe she was. She knew it was more than an honor thing—it was an unfathomable person who existed out there who would put that pucker of skin into his mouth and try to fill her. She knew that the moment might fail, that for all the efforts of anyone, it would still never be enough.

It was her mother who filled her head with Romeo, blind Romeo with the eyes that saw from the heart. "Just one look at your beautiful face. That will tell anyone you are a diamond." She was trying to convince herself a man would think this, that he would marry Claudia and they would have a whirlwind twelve-course Chinese wedding banquet. Her mother didn't believe in the Fong family legend. Not a single person on her side of the family looked funny: they were balanced people, a little on the boring side, but symmetrical just the same. She laughed along with her when Claudia admonished her father's story, and then she'd stop her, telling Claudia to respect him when it had gone on for too long.

Landing in Hong Kong, her father pointed out the beautiful, dark harbor and the city lights that pressed, swollen, around it. And then, pretending he was still talking about it and not his daughter, he said, "Think of the beauty that is still around you, and you be happy!" He was quoting Anne Frank, the only non-Chinese person whom he felt had suffered sufficiently for him to admire.

"I'm okay," she mumbled. Her ears were popping; she was woozy and acted on that feeling. "I'd be happier if I got surgery."

"*Gong chaw ma*—say it again?" His voice went high. "You want to alter what your ancestors gave you?"

They had talked about this before. He had reacted the same way. He looked over at his wife, who was watching Claudia's expression. And her mother worked her magic and pressed her hand against her husband's back, and on the back of his neck, and something in that made him quiet for the rest of the trip.

They took a train into Harbin, a fast rail that shot in a rapid diagonal to the outermost edge of China. The countryside nearing Harbin was peppered with a few red yaks and live-stock. There was little artificial light anywhere in the city itself— lanterns still diffused the morning ice along the market street of Harbin, making the city not a city at all, but a continuity of the wild Shangzhi mountains. As she met Poy, who held a taxi waiting for them, she realized humans had not conquered this quadrant—Harbin was makeshift, but married with an ease to its terrain.

"How are you holding up?" her father asked Poy.

"It is easier now that she is out of the hospital."

"We would have come sooner. Why didn't you tell us it had progressed into this?" her father asked. He was rocking in the seat, nervous and tense, and angry at him.

"Leave Poy be," her mother said sharply. "It was Auntie Yee who refused a doctor all this time. It was her own stubbornness."

It was not a surprise that her father would be prejudiced against Poy upon first glance. Poy's face would be titled *Five Muddy Points*: scissor-point eyebrows, wall-less nose, knuckles without eyes, buggy lips, shallow throat. These forecasted all the doom in a person's destiny, from poverty and dishonesty, to dying an early and painful death. It was a horrible assemblage to her parents, who exchanged worrisome glances, and yet he remained a remarkable sort of handsome to Claudia—inviting features for a finger to trace, a fleshy map of contradictions, both rugged and smooth and dimpled and dark.

He seemed misplaced to her, grinning from ear to ear, wearing a ridiculous woolen, olive, toggled coat with a wreath of acrylic fox hair rimmed around the hood. He took them straight to the wooden flat where his mother and he had lived since his father's death. Auntie Yee's platform bed was in the middle of the living room, and she was in it, propped up on pillows with her long, graying hair fanning out in all directions. A cancer the size of a grapefruit was sitting in her stomach; she would die before they left. Claudia's father rushed over to her side, and as if someone had kicked his knees, he went down on them and put his head on her shoulder. Her mother was crying; she went over to the wall altar and lit incense. Claudia wouldn't have cried at all, but some of it had to do with Auntie Yee being close to her father, who told stories of them stoning cobras in the family village, climbing banyans until the skin on their feet was shredded—but most of her sadness came when her father looked back at her and pointed at Auntie Yee's toes, the six of them. "She is a great woman, this auntie of yours."

Auntie opened her eyes; it was the most she could do. Poy walked over with some pills and put them in her mouth. Claudia was crying—not for the person that was already defeated within Auntie, but for the shame that fell over her for wanting to alter her body. She hated her father in that moment, and she hated her mother for being silent more often than not.

She went into the room that Poy and she were to share, and took off her shirt and her bra, and she fished out all the other expensive, corrective bras, and destroyed them with her Swiss army knife, ribboning the foam pads. She unlatched the window, stung by the crazy kind of cold that blasted into the room, and emptied the remnants of the bras outside. When she turned, Poy was standing there with a quizzical look on his face. His eyes went over her bare chest and then he did the most surprising thing: he looked up into her face and smiled at her as if he hadn't a care in the world. He shuffled over to a drawer, yanked out one of his undershirts, and threw it at her.

She woke early in the mornings. It was too cold, even though she was beneath piles of camel throws. It was Poy who always seemed comfortable, the way he leaned against the drafty windows, hands in pockets, grinning. He took Claudia down to the markets where he worked in nothing but the toggled coat with the funny fox collar and a loose shirt. Together they bought black chickens, and he taught her how to hold their necks down as they were slit. But it was the mornings when the sight of him, asleep on the wooden cot on the other side of the wall, made her teeth clatter. She was even colder watching him, his dark face and scraggly hair, how he wasn't even wearing a shirt beneath the covers, the bare rounds of his shoulders peeking out. Even on this particular morning, when he had told her it was going to be considerably warmer, above the freezing point, she was numb and shaking. She watched him give a sigh, roll over onto his stomach, and throw his arm out at the floor. She went into the living room where she threw her own blankets atop Auntie Yee. She held her aunt's cold fingers and listened to her shallow, butterfly breaths. She massaged her feet and stroked the sixth toe and batted away the stupid notion of it being a genie's lamp. "Auntie," she said. She feared that her auntie would really awaken into consciousness. She was afraid to hear her voice, this woman with the legendary six toes. "Are you in pain, can you feel me?"

Skinny blue branches of veins made a forest along her throat and arms. She did not stir, her eyes did not move.

"I am Claudia, only daughter of Xiao Fong. I live in Canada, where it's cold but not nearly as bad as here. I go to Longshore High School. I think your son is very … intriguing." She put her head close to her aunt's face, smelling the Tiger Balm ointment that was slathered along her throat.

Claudia didn't want to tell her father what he probably already knew, that Auntie Yee herself had a lucky face, and look what sort of good it did her. Those Fong barbarians were just that, barbarians. They had six toes because they were wild beasts living in the forest, and civilization had the gumption to believe it was an honor. When she put her hand to Auntie Yee's heart, it was barely there, struggling and drowning, falling deeper and deeper within.

Poy wanted to get away from the house. "I'm a bad boy," he said to her. "You want to see?" And he took Claudia's hand, running her past frozen hills bowing forward in waves, opposing one another in a tidal feud. Other times, the land was flat and filled with rust weed for miles. He brought her to the edge of the train tracks where they waited to see the great Trans-Siberia roar past into neighboring Vladivostok. "Me, I love trains—trains move like snakes."

"Nothing wrong with that, Poy. Why are you bad?"

"Listen," he put his finger to his lips. He put his mittened hand on her head and brought it to his. He pointed in the direction of the hills and suddenly the train came blasting through, red and black streaked, curving along the ridge. He gave a great war cry, waving his hands at it. "You see, you see. I will get on that train, and ride it forever."

"When?"

"Soon." His face was suddenly in a frown.

"You're not bad for wanting it," she found herself saying. She looked up, watching formations of blackened birds tear up the sky, which seemed ripped in places.

Each afternoon they stood at the far end of the train platform and waited for its arrival. She imagined riding it with Poy, taking notice through smoked windows the growth of industrial muck creeping into Chinese pastures, cement factories rising up from the hard frozen mud in whorls like cake icing. It was the coldest month of the year, but it wouldn't matter because she imagined they'd be in the warmest car packed with all of the third-class passengers—workers that would stop just before crossing into Russian territory. On the boarding platform, passengers wailed in the cold wearing fifteen layers—thick, padded *minops* over woolen scarf-like wraps that twisted and wound around their bodies like giant gift bows. They were mostly an impoverished lot, haggard faces bent into newspapers. Sometimes, in anticipation of boarding, Claudia could see the flash of pink, the loosening of a denture jut from an old man's mouth just before he sucked it back in. Her heart froze, watching what plastic teeth could do, faking the face. From the outside, the passengers seemed an endless window of compressed swans, flesh pressed to white, combustible.

Poy was always saddened. They had watched the trains for a week, and on Friday he refused to watch the train pull out of the station. He put his head on her shoulder, and she could smell his skin, sandalwood and incense like hers. He took hold of her sleeve, pulling his hood over his head and fastening the ties. "I don't want to hear the whistle, I can't bear it any longer, I don't want to hear it. "

"Let's go then," she said.

They started to run from the platform, moving past the enamel doors that buzzed wide, and down the steep path which was frozen over. "You think I'm strange, ah?" He started to laugh.

She shook her head.

"I'm tired of watching the trains go," he said slowly. "It's a bad habit. Mother used to take me to see the trains all the time when I was a boy."

And she saw her auntie, her hands slipping down Poy's

shoulders and lifting him up into the air. She saw them caught together in the heat of the train, the steam billowing out from its belly—and then she saw incense smoke rising from crumbled ash, and her auntie's head cradled between two pillows, the back of her skull balanced atop a lacquered wood block. They were halfway down the path, when the high shrill of the whistle sounded from above. Poy kept running, veering them off the path and onto the lawns, where they crunched through knee-deep ice.

They spent the rest of the day at the famous Ice Lantern Festival in Zhaolin Park. The crowds were enormous, dressed in thick, bright *minops* maneuvering past a world of sculpted ice. Old men brought their birds perched in bamboo domes out to sun. Claudia walked arm in arm with Poy, adoring laughing babies smacking their palms, hair like dandelions caught in water, doused in winter sun. They walked through ice castles, sitting in frosted thrones, petting chiseled parrots behind chandelier cages. Everyone was quilted and smiling and eating red-bean desserts served over shaved ice.

Poy was drinking Tsing Tsao beers that he fit into his coat pockets. His body was wild, snapping forward, kissing the ice animals. In the reflection of the sculptures, their lucky and unlucky faces were mangled just the same. He began to dance, throwing his arms above his head and bowing before an island of buxom mermaids.

"I will ride the Trans-Siberia all the way to Canada!"

"It doesn't go to Canada, Poy."

"I'll bribe the conductor."

"How will you know where to look for me?"

"I will just tell him to look for my cousin with the lucky face and prosperous nose." And he kissed her there, on the flat end of her nose. He threw his head back, laughing so hard the steam bloomed as a cirrus from his mouth. Poy, as naive as he seemed, was of the bigger world, had the harder edge. As crazy as he was, he was heavy in this place. A small crowd gathered to cheer him on, clapping through mittens as he started to dance again. Poy thrust his hand out at Claudia, and together they started to waltz. It was long and exaggerated, Poy swinging them into the crowd so that they drew back, trailing behind. She felt faces sweeping past her, their movements as intricate as if they were tracing a doily. She could identify each frozen animal as it passed her; she could look up into the sky and see ribbons, a line of lanterns and a ceiling of smoke that boxed them in. Then Poy whipped them around and they broke open, holding onto one hand, the other suspended, searching to be found. She envied the way his body could unravel, renouncing the cold—she pulled her mitten off, stretched her free arm as high as it could reach, testing the expanse of the night, her naked hand struck with blindness.

She loved him right then, without an explanation, without a care.

Auntie Yee was gone by the time they returned. They were heading up the path and saw the door open, incense smoke churning out. The incense burned their eyes as they entered the house, her father pushing them down to their knees. "Bow," he ordered. "Where were you both, how could you be so careless?"

"She is making her passage to the afterworld," her mother said.

Her aunt was already dressed in her best gown, a chocolate silk embroidered with turquoise phoenixes. Her eyes were closed, her arms were crossed over her breast. Claudia tightened her grip around Poy's arm, but he was stoic. He bowed deeply three times, and got up to relight the candles. He retrieved a pail and started a small fire in it, and then he started to burn lucky money envelopes, giving his mother money to spend in the afterworld. Claudia and her parents kneeled until the monks came to take her body to the temple.

The bed remained in the center of the flat, incense smoke ascending from all four posters. Her mother gathered up the throws and rolled them into neat bundles, her fingers working quickly. There was a layer of chill still hovering across the floor from the doors being flung open. Claudia's father rose from his knees and he walked over to Poy, who was hunched over on a stool. He brought his foot up on one of the rungs, and presented Poy with an envelope. "Before we arrived, I made a decision to purchase this plane ticket. You're a grown boy. I cannot make the decision for you to come."

Poy took the envelope with both hands, looking at it carefully, nodding graciously up at Claudia's parents. He smiled and it revealed his dimples and the creases at the corners of his eyes and, Claudia knew, her parents foolishly believed he was coming. Perhaps it was the deception his face emanated, perhaps this was why her father would gaze upon it and declare it unlucky. Poy turned and smiled at her, but for her he let his brows furrow, and she was struck with his sadness.

That night she asserted her decision by clenching her fists, and crept into Poy's bed. She rubbed her hands together to make them warm, and she put them on his cheeks. He was silent, not moving for the longest time. And then he got up on his elbows and lifted his head, placing it back down into her neck. She felt his wet face, how he was trembling. She felt fortunate in that moment; she knew to savor the sadness, and the coiled lock they had on one another. He ran his hand over her face, and then he sighed, as if realizing something, going beneath her shirt, and placing his hand over the pucker of skin. His fingers did not mean to cover, like so many other hands might have wished to—and though they were blind in the cold darkness, she knew Poy held a smile despite the concourse of his unlucky face.

"I was born like this," she whispered. "Missing."

"No. Simply unknown, a wonderful mystery. I call it the other."

"Tell me, Poy," she asked, "what are you going to do with the ticket?"

"Keep it in this dresser drawer, maybe for later, maybe for not ever."

"Isn't unknown the same thing as missing?"

And she knew from his silence that it was not. She realized she had not thought of her absent breast for a while until that moment, and even then, it felt real against his hand. She wondered about those barbaric Fongs, running amok in the forest with their sixth toes getting caught on twigs, tripping up the way they walked, and of Auntie Yee, who probably wobbled painfully down the hills. She felt sorry for her father, who was probably jealous. She slept with her face pressed to Poy's—she had never felt something so warm entangled around her. There was an impermanence about them that made the moment feel safe. And when she thought a piece of clarity would finally enter her, it was hardly that, but the feeling of vastness.

An offering plate of food needed to be made the next day for her aunt's ceremonies. She went down to the market alone, selecting a black hen that was neither plump nor gaunt, going against her father's instructions—she was sure her auntie would want an unassuming, modest-looking hen. She selected sweet buns that were sprinkled with coconut, and *tsa siu*, glazed pork cut into slivers. She went back to the flat and pressed the hen down on the tree stump, and her father ran the blade of a knife through its neck.

"Your auntie taught me this, how to end a life without it feeling pain." He fixed his eyes on the stump, awkward. "We did many things, and then we grew apart, for years and years."

She nodded at her father. It was the longest thing he had said to her since they arrived in Harbin.

"I regret that now."

"She is watching you, Dad. I know she is. I don't know her, not like you do. I know her in a different way, how you always say I'm like her. I know her like a dream."

"Which is why you are lucky."

She shook her head, but he didn't see her. She scooped up the hen and carried it back into the house to pluck it. She went over to the window and saw the ring of chicken blood around the chopping stump. The color washed out towards the edge, concentric like the cloudy bands of agate. She waited for Poy's figure to emerge from the roadside, the beastly, hirsute shadows of his fox collar creeping across the ground.

Steven Polansky

1955. Squeezing out "Lady of Spain," the only song I knew. Teaching a child to play the accordion is like teaching him Estonian. I no longer play, though from time to time I tip our piano on end and have a go.

Steven Polansky's short stories have appeared in the *New Yorker, Harper's,* the *New England Review,* and elsewhere. His story "Leg" was included in *The Best American Short Stories, 1995.* He lives in Minnesota with his wife and two sons, and is working on his second novel.

STEVEN POLANSKY

Rein

*J*ay Ephraim and Peter Findlay were old friends, who had not seen one another in twenty-five years.

Jay Ephraim was a Jew from the Queens public schools. Peter Findlay, from the Upper Peninsula of Michigan and Palm Springs, went to prep school in Massachusetts. In college together, both studied English literature. Jay wrote his senior paper on the unabridged *Clarissa*, Peter on Tennyson's *Idylls of the King*. Two years after graduation Jay married Lucy Hutchins, a dance major from Virginia, whom Peter had dated first. Jay and Lucy were still married and lived in Sparta, Wisconsin, where Jay taught in the high school. Lucy did not work. She was chronically ill. They had one child—a son, Eli, who was eleven.

After college, Jay and Peter did not correspond, until late summer of this year, two weeks before Jay's term at the high school was to start, when Peter, who split his time between ranches he owned in Michigan and Arizona, sent Jay a small book, *Think Harmony with Horses*, written by the western trainer Ray Hunt. Stuck to the front cover was a Post-it note with a handwritten sentence lifted from the book's first paragraph: "If you find a friend in life before somebody else finds him, you're real lucky."

Glimmer Train Stories, Issue 25, Winter 1998
©*1997 Steven Polansky*

Because it came from Peter, Jay read the book at once. It was repetitive and roughsawn. It set forth a view of life as horsemanship, a so-called equesology, in which the right relation of man to horse was posed as the key to right living. The first paragraph, which Jay thought the best and sufficient, ended: "But every horse you ride can be your friend because you ask this of them. This is real important to me. You can ask the horse to do your thing, but you ask him; you offer it to him in a good way. You fix it up and let him find it."

For all Peter's inherited wealth, sophistication, and ambition, he had always been a cowboy. He was chivalrous, sentimental, slow to speak. And he could ride. He and Jay had ridden, sometimes twice a week, at a stable half an hour's drive from campus where Peter kept Grand River Jack, a reining horse with regal bloodlines. They drove there in Peter's pickup—he owned, too, a leaf green Porsche 911—with Squire, Peter's blue heeler, in the bed. The dog went everywhere with Peter, including class. Jay rode one of the stable's trail horses, an Appaloosa named Red, on days the old pole bender was up to it. Jay had learned English seat at summer camp. He could not sit a trot and had invariably to shorten his stirrups. In bad weather, Jay had been happy to watch Peter work Grand River Jack in the arena. Around horses Peter was intuitive and deft. By conventional measures Jay was the better student, but he wondered, then and now, if he would ever, in any aspect of his own life, be so competent or graceful. He'd shown, sadly, no special gifts as a husband. If he had not actually caused Lucy's disintegration, he had found nothing to do to prevent it. He might have made a good father, but Eli needed little guidance. The child was delivered sensible and smart, and developed quickly into a steady, compassionate person. Jay and Lucy mused about where on earth he'd come from. Eli had, Peter was to tell Jay, what the Indians called an old soul.

Peter followed his gift of the book with a phone call. He was in Nebraska, en route from Arizona to Michigan, trailering four horses. He planned to leave two of them in Wisconsin, at the university in River Falls. He'd contracted with a man there in equine studies—not coincidentally a Ray Hunt disciple, who was now, to Peter's mind, himself the master—to train his two-year-olds. If it was convenient for Jay and for Lucy, Peter said, he would stop for a visit that next afternoon. Were they free? Hearing Peter's voice made Jay almost giddy. They were free, Jay told him.

When Peter called, Lucy was in bed. It was late afternoon. Eli was outside on his roller blades, working up and down the block on his backward crossovers, thinking about hockey. He was studious about the skills involved, though it was a game for which he lacked the requisite aggression. Jay went up to the bedroom, concerned he had not asked Lucy before he told Peter to come by. He did not want to see her angry. "Are you awake?" Jay said. The curtains were drawn and, though hours of daylight were left, the room was nearly dark.

"Yes," she said.

Jay sat down on the bed beside her. She had covered her eyes with the edge of a pillow. On her night table were two mugs, a tin of throat lozenges, lip balm, aspirin, a roll of toilet paper, her glasses, a washcloth, a spray of silk flowers in a squat, narrow-mouthed vase, and a small stack of paperback mysteries. "Did the phone ring?" she said.

"You won't believe who it was." She didn't respond.

"Peter Findlay," he said.

She smiled. "Hmmn," she said, as if she were falling asleep.

"He's in Nebraska," Jay said. "He called from his truck." He moved the pillow away from her face so he could see her eyes.

"Don't," she said.

"He's coming here tomorrow afternoon."

"I'm getting up," she said. She stretched her arms out to either side, made a faint noise in her throat.

"Now?" he said.

"Soon," she said. "In a bit."

She was not angry.

"Do you want dinner?" he said.

"No," she said.

Jay put his hand on her forehead, as if he were feeling for fever. Her skin was cool and dry. He brushed the hair off her face. Her hair had gone gray, her face was sharp and drawn. She was no longer beautiful. "I'll take Eli out for something," he said.

"Okay," she said.

"Then I'll be back."

"Okay," she said.

Jay was sorry he'd married her. For whatever reasons—he could supply a deplorably varied list—she was, married to him, more and more often miserable. It was not, he believed, because she did not love him. Nor was it something about marriage, essentially, that had driven her crazy. Her neurochemicals were out of sync—the clinical diagnosis—*and* it was he. Something about him, something about being married to him in reaction with her psychopathology, that caused, over the long term—twenty-two years—a debilitating become incapacitating anger and grief. Rage was a word he'd learned to use. What was she rageful about? What was she grieving? She couldn't tell you. He couldn't say exactly, or briefly, though he could circle it, and circle it, until he got near enough the discouraging heart.

Jay and Eli went for dinner to a Chinese restaurant Eli liked. When they'd ordered, Jay offered Eli quarters for the video games in the vestibule. "No thanks," Eli said.

"Go ahead."

"No thanks."

Eli was a beautiful boy with—Jay's mother had said this too many times for anyone's comfort—a beautiful Jewish face: the sharpness, the lack of fineness in Jay's features, through Lucy softened there and refined. Eli was dark, with long delicate fingers and prehensile lashes that, to his embarrassment, had caused a stewardess to say, "We could roast marshmallows on those." Though, ostensibly, Eli was big and strong enough to handle himself, there was a generalized softness and delicacy about him, a maturity of pace and tone that made it tough for him with boys his own age.

"Your mom's in bed today," Jay said.

"I know," Eli said. "She's in the dumps."

"What makes you say that?"

"I know it. She is."

"I mean," Jay said, "where did you get the expression, 'in the dumps'?"

"I don't know," Eli said. "Probably I read it."

"You're a good reader."

"I guess."

"That's a thing about you that makes me happy," Jay said. "What are you reading these days?"

"*Prince Caspian.*"

"I don't know that," Jay said. "Good?"

Eli nodded, then turned inward. It was a visible shift, and Jay figured he was either thinking about his book or trying to decide what conversational move would next be most respectful.

"What are you reading?" Eli said.

"Oh, a book about horses."

Eli made a face meant to reassure Jay his choice of books was acceptable, then said, "What kind of horses?"

"About how to train them," Jay said. "An old friend of mine sent it to me."

"Sounds good," Eli said.

"He's my old, old friend. His name is Peter. He's coming tomorrow. He'll have horses with him."

"He will?"

"Four. And some dogs, I'll bet you."

"Does he know who I am?" Eli said.

"He does. He can't wait to meet you."

"I will like to meet him, too," Eli said.

Eli liked to touch his food. Whatever he ate he first touched in a dreamy, sensual, almost obsessive way that made Jay tense. Eli rested his wrist on the rim of his plate, his fingers dangled above his food, the tips of his fingers playing lightly on the rice, lemon chicken, snowpeas, water chestnuts. He touched each bit of food before he put it in his mouth. Turned it over in his fingers, pinched it, squared it, patted it, paid it loving, if subconscious attention. He was not testing the food—this was clear—but apprehending it in a tactile way before he smelled or tasted it.

"Use your fork," Jay said. "For God's sake."

"Sorry."

"You're too old for that."

Eli picked up his fork. "Sorry," he said.

"Okay," Jay said.

Eli ate a piece of chicken, then put his fork down. "I guess I'm done," he said.

"You're not hungry?" Jay said.

"No."

"You want to take it home?"

"No," Eli said. "What about Mom?"

"She didn't want anything. I asked her."

"What will *she* eat?" Eli said.

"I don't know," Jay said. "I can fix her something. Hey. Are you looking forward to school starting?"

"Either way."

"What about hockey?"

"Maybe I won't play," Eli said.

"Why not?"

"I don't know," Eli said. "I don't want to think about it right now."

Lucy was wild when Jay and Eli got home. They stood just inside the front door, at the bottom of the staircase. They could hear and feel her thumping around upstairs. She slammed a door. She was running back and forth above their heads. They heard her turn on the bathtub faucet full bore, then abruptly shut it off. She slammed the bathroom door. They saw her whisk by the top of the stairs. She had her hands to her face. She did not stop or look down at them.

"Eli," Jay said. "I want you to go watch TV. Right now."

"There's nothing on," Eli said.

"Do it," Jay said.

"I'll read," Eli said.

"No," Jay said. "You turn on the TV."

"Fine," Eli said.

In the kitchen Jay made some toast and tea and quartered an orange. Lucy continued to thrash and flail upstairs. There was a loud thud, as if she'd fallen out of bed, that rattled the ceiling fixture in the kitchen. Usually it was hard to tell what it was, exactly, that set her off. Jay assumed she was hungry. Maybe she was angry with him, after she'd had a chance to think it over, about Peter.

Jay went upstairs with the toast and the tea and the orange.

She was in the bedroom, on the bed, on her knees. Her nose was bleeding, and she was stanching it with her nightdress. She looked at him as he came in the room. She was bouncing on her knees. "I will not touch your feet," she said. She shook her head violently. "Fucker. No. Get your shoes away from my face."

"All right," Jay said. "I will. What happened to your nose?"

"Where?" she said. She looked at the front of her nightdress, which was splattered with blood. "It's bleeding. Did you do this, Pumpkin?"

"I've brought you some tea and toast," Jay said. "Are you hungry? You must be hungry."

"I was running. I banged my nose."

"I can see that," Jay said. He sat beside her on the bed. She stopped bouncing. He put his hand gently on the side of her neck, beneath her ear. She leaned into his hand and closed her eyes. "Heaven," she said.

"Do me a favor, Luce?"

"What?"

"Eli's downstairs," he said. "Don't shout."

She lay face down on the bed, her head at the foot. He spread his palm gently on her back. She was sweating. He could feel her spine. They were quiet for a full five minutes.

"I'm famished," she said.

"I've brought you some tea and toast. And an orange."

"Thank you," she said. "Where were you?"

"I took Eli for dinner."

"Is he okay?" she said.

"He's fine."

"Does he want to see me?" she said.

"Maybe a little later," Jay said.

"He shouldn't see me," she said. Then, "The good boy."

"You can clean up. Come down."

"I will," she said. "I will come down."

Jay reached over to the night table and tore off a wad of toilet paper. "Use this," he said. "You'll spoil your clothes."

She held the toilet paper to her nose. "Is Peter Findlay coming?" she said.

"Yes. Tomorrow afternoon sometime. Is that okay?"

Lucy thought a moment. "It will be good to see him," she said.

The next afternoon at four, Peter called from Camelot Cleaners in town.

"How long have you been there?" Jay said.

"An hour."

"Why didn't you call?"

"I was doing the wash. Did you want to watch?"

"Hell yes," Jay said.

"Come on, then," Peter said.

Jay first went upstairs to see Lucy. She was sitting on the chair in their bedroom, in a camisole with a small blue flower embroidered at the neck. Jay had always liked the way she looked in this. She was still, staring at the pair of white cotton anklets in her hands. "Lucy," Jay said softly.

The socks flew out of her hands, sideways, in opposite directions. "You scared me," she said.

"Peter just called."

"I didn't hear the ring," she said. She gathered her socks and tried to put them on. "Where is he?"

"He's in town. He stopped to do his laundry."

"Oh," she said. "No. Why? I could have done that for him here."

"I'm going to get him. Are you okay?"

"Come on. Hush. But shall I fix something?"

"Whatever you want. Iced tea would be nice. Or lemonade. Some cookies."

"What were those cookies he liked to eat?" she said.

"Peter?"

"He liked to eat those cookies."

"I don't remember," he said. "It doesn't matter. Whatever you have."

Several blocks off, Jay could see the long silver trailer. It was as if a car of a train had come uncoupled in front of the cleaners. Peter was folding the last of his wash. He saw Jay and, holding a pair of boxers, came outside to meet him.

"I don't want your underwear," Jay said.

The two men hugged, then shook hands. Jay rubbed Peter's arm near the shoulder. "It is good to see you," Jay said.

"You too," Peter said.

Jay stepped back. "You look good." He shook his head.

"What?" Peter said.

"Nothing. You look great."

Jay found himself moved, and a bit shaken, by how good Peter looked. Peter was thin and hard. His face, though marked by age, was still fine. In the August heat, Peter wore jeans, a starched blue oxford-cloth shirt buttoned at the neck and wrists, and a pair of coffee-colored ropers. His hair, in college the color of straw, had taken a deeper gold. Jay knew that he himself had not aged so well. He had gotten a trace ponderous and jowly and had begun to lose his hair. He wondered how Peter saw him. He was tempted to apologize. "You must be wrung out."

"Not bad," Peter said. When they heard Peter's voice, the horses began to shuffle and snort. "They're not happy. I need to water them."

"Can you do that at my house?"

"If you've got a hose," Peter said.

"Eli will flip."

"Your boy."

"You'll like him," Jay said. "How come no dogs? I'm surprised."

"They're around," Peter said. He opened the door to the cleaners and gave a clipped whistle. Three dogs, of varying size, tore out, tumbling all over themselves, jostling for Peter's attention.

"My girls," Peter said. He picked up the littlest one—a piebald and wirehaired mongrel—by the scruff of the neck and held her at eye-level. "I found this one in the desert. She was pretty much gone." He put the dog down, and it set to wholehearted scratching. "The other two are with me longer.

That one," he pointed to the largest of the three, "Rosie, is part coyote. She's dead shy."

Jay crouched and clicked his tongue. "Rosie," he said. "C'mere girl." The dog sidled towards him then veered off.

Peter opened the passenger door of the pickup, and the dogs piled in. "How's Lucy?" Peter said.

"She's okay," Jay said.

"Good."

"You'll see her," Jay said.

"Good," Peter said. "I'll follow you."

Parked in front of Jay's house, Peter's trailer was a spectacle. The kids in bathing suits across the street stopped running through the sprinkler and gaped. The Norwegian woman, whose name Jay could not pronounce, came out onto her front porch. Eli was in the driveway with his hockey stick shooting tennis balls at the garage door.

"Eli," Jay said, "this is Peter, my friend."

"Eli," Peter said.

"Hi," Eli said. "Nice to meet you." He shook hands with Peter and tried to look him in the eye, as Jay had asked him to, but the trailer was irresistible.

"Are your horses in there?" Eli said.

"Four," Jay said. "Peter needs you to help water them."

"What do I do?" Eli said.

"Stay right here," Peter said. He took a black rubberized bucket from the back of the trailer. "Can you fill this with water?"

"Yes," Eli said.

"He can do that," Jay said.

Peter's dogs were making short, tentative dashes, sniffing the bottoms of bushes, nipping at one another. They seemed to intuit the limits of Jay's yard and did not go past them.

"You have these dogs, too?" Eli said.

"I do," Peter said.

"What's this one's name?" Eli pointed at the coyote.

"Rosie," Peter said. "That one is Julia. She's my old girl. The little rat is Gwen."

Eli laughed.

"I asked her," Peter said. "That's what she wanted to be called."

Eli put down the bucket and kneeled on the sidewalk. The coyote came to him and shoved her nose between his knees. Eli scratched her behind the ears. The dog lifted her head and smiled.

"Hey," Eli said, "she smiled."

"She does that," Peter said. "When she's happy."

"Will you take the horses out?" Eli asked.

"I will," Peter said, "One at a time, or we'll have a stampede."

"That would be cool," Eli said.

"It wouldn't," Peter said. "You fill the bucket, and I'll get one of those guys out so he can drink."

Jay went with Eli around the back of the house to the garden spigot. "Did you see your mother?" Jay said.

"No," Eli said.

"Did she come downstairs, do you know?"

"I don't know," Eli said. "Will he let me ride one?"

"I doubt it," Jay said. "Ask him."

When they'd filled the bucket, Jay left Eli to carry it out front, and he went in the back door. He moved quickly through the first floor, calling Lucy's name. There was no answer. He wanted to be outside with Peter and Eli, to watch them together.

He ran up the stairs. At the top he called again, "Lucy." There was still no answer. She was in bed, with the curtains drawn and the lights out. "What's going on?" Jay said.

"Hi," she said.

"Peter's here. What's going on?"

"Is Peter Findlay finally here?" she said. Then she laughed at the sounds she'd made.

"Yes. He is."

"Is he in the house?"

"He's outside with Eli. They're watering the horses."

Lucy laughed again.

"What's funny?"

"Like nasturtiums," she said.

"That's how they say it," Jay said. "What's going on here now?"

"I know you mean with me."

"Why are you in bed? I thought you'd be down. We talked about iced tea. Can you remember? We talked about the cookies."

"I don't think I can do it," she said. "Don't be angry."

"What don't you think you can do?"

"I don't think I can see Peter today."

"Why not? He's eager to see you. He asked how you were."

"What did you say?"

"I don't know. I said you were good. I said you were good."

"I'm a mess," she said.

"Get dressed," he said. "Comb your hair. You'll be fine."

"You're sweet," she said. "To me."

"I don't feel sweet."

"Be sweet." She started to cry, then stopped. "Be sweet," she said. "I don't think I'll come down."

"Please. Lucy. Don't do this. Come down. Get dressed. See Peter."

"Not today," she said. "Next time."

"What next time? No. We haven't seen him in twenty-five years. What are you talking about?"

"I'm not making sense," she said. "How does Peter look?"

"He looks terrific. Come see for yourself."

"I don't think so."

"Damn it," Jay said. "Don't do this." He kicked a shoe—his heavy brogue beside the bed—across the room.

Inadvertently, he lifted it. It smacked against the mirror above the vanity, then fell into the sink.

"Leave me," Lucy said.

"Plain wacko," Jay said.

"You leave me," Lucy said.

"I'm going down," Jay said.

Down the middle of the street, coming towards him, Jay saw Peter leading his chestnut colt with Eli astride. They were followed by an entourage—the kids in bathing suits and three skateboarders who had been drawn in. Peter held the lead rope slackly, not looking back at the colt. Jay resisted shouting, "Careful." Except for a red saddle blanket, Eli rode bareback. He had a handful of mane and sat bent-legged, knees high on the colt's neck, like a jockey. The colt seemed calm, glad to be out and moving, and walked easily, even with the kids capering at his heels and the skateboarders swooping up and down driveways to maintain their speed. Eli was smiling. He had not been on a horse before. Jay could hear the regular, clean sound of the colt's hooves against the pavement. As he got close, he could hear Peter talking to Eli about feeling the colt through his legs.

"How is it?" Jay said.

"Great," Eli said. "This is the greatest horse." Jay walked beside Peter. He watched Eli, ready to catch him should he fall.

"He might well be," Peter said.

"He's a good one?" Jay said.

"Could be real good."

"It's nice of you to let him ride."

"No. He needs to deal with someone else on him. I wanted to see how he'd react."

"Any appreciable risk?" Jay said.

Peter laughed. "Not appreciable. He knows I'm watching him."

"You got yourself a troop," Jay said.

"He's good and steady."

Back in front of the house, Eli slid off the colt. Peter coaxed the horse into the trailer and backed another one out, a compact bay filly with a star on her forehead and a snip on her muzzle. "His sister," Peter said. He made the kids clear a broad space. "She can be snaky," he said to Jay.

The filly drank noisily. "The lady," Peter said.

"Let me tell you this now," Jay said. "Lucy won't come down."

Peter looked at Jay but said nothing. "She's in her bedroom," Jay said. "I just spoke with her." Jay glanced up at the bedroom window and saw, shadowed behind the screen, Lucy's face. He looked away. "She's not doing especially well," Jay said. He hoped Peter had not seen her.

Eli stood apart with the skateboarders. "I don't want him to hear this," Jay said.

"Sure," Peter said.

"She said to tell you how sorry she was."

"I'm sorry, too," Peter said.

"I know," Jay said.

Jay turned his back to Eli. "I don't know what to say," he said.

"Eli," Peter said. "Find me a ball you don't want. We'll give the dogs a game."

Eli started up the driveway. The coyote and Gwen went with him. The old dog stuck close to Peter.

"No, but she's real down right now," Jay said. "She doesn't feel presentable. She doesn't want to be seen. I guess she doesn't want you, of all people, to see her."

Peter led the filly away from the bucket. "That's enough,"

he said to the horse. Then, to Jay, "Let's finish up out here. Then we'll go in and talk. It's all right if I come in?"

"Of course," Jay said. "I'll tell you what. I'm useless. You finish. I'll go make us something to drink."

"No need," Peter said.

"I'm happy to do it," Jay said.

Jay and Peter sat on the screened porch, which looked out on the backyard, narrow and deep, where Eli played with the dogs. Jay made a pitcher of iced tea from an envelope mix and discovered some shortbread cookies, which he set on a salad plate. They talked for an hour, every so often stopping to watch a trick Eli had devised for Gwen. They tried to catch up. Peter told Jay that ten years ago he had married a woman with two children nearly grown. It had been a vexed marriage and had recently ended. Although he did not speak to their mother, Peter kept in touch with the children, both of whom were now in college. He talked to Jay about his work breeding, training, showing, and selling reining horses—quarter horses bred and trained to perform gymnastic western maneuvers, stylized for the show ring. Jay spoke briefly about his teaching. They tried to remember what they'd read, in common, in college. Then Jay told Peter what had happened to Lucy, as he understood it.

When Jay had finished, Peter sat silent for a time. Then he said, "What will you do?"

"Beats me," Jay said. "What do they say? Abide. Ride it out."

Peter said nothing.

"No pun intended," Jay said.

Peter had to get to River Falls in time to talk with his trainer and stable his horses. Eli came in to say goodbye. He stood with Jay and Peter in the front hall, at the foot of the stairs. "You're a good hand with dogs," Peter said to the boy.

"I like them," Eli said. "Gwen is so smart. Thanks for bringing them."

"Peter will be back," Jay said. "You'll see him tomorrow."

"I will?" Eli said.

Peter nodded.

"Will you bring your horses?"

"Two of them."

"The one I rode?"

"No," Peter said. "He needs schooling. Right now he's dumb."

"He is not," Eli said. "You're teasing."

"I am," Peter said. "But he does need work if he wants to be a champion."

"Will he be?" Eli said.

"You rode him," Peter said. "What do you think?"

"I think he will," Eli said.

There was a rustling above them.

"Mom," Eli said.

Lucy was at the top of the stairs. She was holding her bathrobe closed at the chest, sitting way down on her haunches, scrunched up, as if she were trying to be as small as possible. Her hair was unpinned and fell across her face.

"Peter," she said. "Hello. Hello."

"Lucy," Peter said.

"I can't see you," she said. "Did Jay tell you?"

"Yes," Peter said. He put a foot on the stairs.

"Don't come up," she said.

Peter withdrew his foot. "I wouldn't," he said.

"I'm sick," she said.

"I'm sorry," Peter said.

"Did Jay tell you?"

"Yes," Peter said.

"It's true," she said.

Peter looked up at her. She brushed the hair from her eyes. Jay opened the front door. "Go outside," he said to Eli. The boy complied.

"Peter Findlay," she said.

Peter smiled.

"It is wonderful to see you," she said.

"You too," he said.

The next day, as they'd agreed, Jay met Peter at the horse

barn in River Falls. They stood together outside the ring and watched the trainer, Tom Morgan, work Peter's horses. The day was hot when Jay arrived late morning. The ring was shaded by several large cottonwood trees. Inside the fence the earth was soft and a deep brown. Peter left six of his colts year-round with Morgan, than whom, Peter told Jay, there was no better trainer anywhere. On top of his duties for the university as Head Herdsman, Morgan rode each of Peter's colts daily. Morgan was unprepossessing, even on horseback. He wore a dull blue flannel shirt, jeans, and a black baseball cap with the name of Peter's most profitable stud on the front. He had a sweet, peachy face. There was nothing cowboyish about him. He looked to Jay like a man who might work in a dairy.

As he was saddling a filly named Vivien's Kid, Morgan told Jay about a beautiful woman who regularly called him to help load her horse into her trailer.

"In this business," Morgan said, "you see a lot of damsels in distress. Real Zane Grey." Morgan was not bragging. He was sympathetic, quietly amused. "She had a couple of trailer wrecks, I guess." He checked the cinch, tugged on the stirrup, then got on the horse. It was a slow, looping, weightless move. He shifted himself in the saddle, then turned the filly in a tight circle.

"The lady just happens to be beautiful," Morgan said. "I'd do the same for the fat, ugly ones."

Jay asked him how much he charged.

"She'd pay whatever I ask," he said. "Fifty dollars. A hundred." He leaned forward to scratch the filly behind the ear. "It's a power no man should have," he said.

Peter had come to see how his colts had progressed. Morgan worked them in different gaits, mostly trots and lopes, taking them through rollbacks, changes of lead, stops, gentle spins.

He talked continuously to Peter. He told him what he was doing and, move by move, what the horse was thinking. The operative assumption, Jay saw, was that Morgan was inside the colt's head, thinking in harmony. Even when the horse did not deliver, Morgan was patient and happy.

"She's the most contrary of the bunch," he said of Vivien's Kid. "There was very little willingness yesterday. I got a twisted wire in her. I don't always do that, but sometimes I do. She sure wants to stop, and today she wants to go."

Even at the far end of the ring, Morgan spoke at a conversational pitch. "Can you hear what he's saying?" Jay asked Peter.

"I know what he's saying," Peter said.

Morgan was particularly sanguine about a colt named Melody's Lightning. "He's got a nice look. He's pretty fresh. Wouldn't hurt if I turned him loose first." Morgan laid the reins down on the pommel. He took a pair of leather gloves out of his back pocket and put them on. As he picked up the reins, the colt, unbidden, started off.

"For a minute here I'm just gonna go with him. He's not quite to the stage where you want to channel all this. He's probably the most purely energetic of the whole group. He does like to go somewhere. He's almost had to learn how to trot. He's wanted to do that funny little shuffle. He'd way rather lope. And so what I do when he's this fresh, when he's loping and I want him to trot, I don't ask him to trot, I just let him find the trot. He'll trot real good. See there. See what he did? He did not want to think about going level. He's gonna be a fancy horse."

Morgan took the colt through a lead change that was, to Jay, imperceptible. "Did you see that?" Morgan asked Peter.

"Could barely see it," Peter said. "That was pretty."

"Yeah," Morgan said. "He's gonna be fancy. All I do is just pull till I get a step right. But I can't do that until some of the

58

freshness is gone. I'm just gonna lope here until he comes into a trot himself. He's in a good frame of mind. Watch this."

He took one hand off the rein. Without any discernible goad, the colt lined up his feet and found a comfortable trot. "He's the real deal. This is a very good day because when I line him up he is straight, straight, straight."

Morgan brought the horse to a stop, then asked him to move backwards. "He's pretty uncoordinated backing up. His hind end and his front end just aren't hooked up yet. But he'll be fine."

Peter explained that Morgan practiced resistance-free training. "Did you read that book I sent you?" Peter said.

"I did read it," Jay said.

"Because here it is," Peter said.

Morgan heard this exchange and laughed. "Hell, no," he said. "I found the answer. Just beat 'em up and spur 'em one day, then ride 'em the next."

When Peter had seen his colts, the three men went to lunch at the North Fork Cafe, a hangout for students and horsemen on the broad main street of River Falls. They sat at a round table in the back of the cafe, away from the windows. The cafe was not air conditioned, but it was cool and quiet. The lunch crowd had gone. The food was passable. For most of the meal the talk was of horses and, more spiritedly, of horse trainers. Tom Morgan did much of the talking, though it was clear in the way he spoke—not obsequious, but with an unfaltering respect—that the horses in his charge were Peter's.

It was only when Morgan left for the barn that Peter and Jay were able to speak about Lucy.

It was Jay who brought her up. There was something he wanted to ask Peter. "Go ahead." Peter said.

"This is awkward," Jay said. He spread his palms on the table, thumbs hooked beneath, as if he were holding his balance.

"Well, that's all right," Peter said.

Jay looked around. It was a gratuitously furtive gesture. There was no one. "I guess what I'm wondering is about you and Lucy."

Peter nodded. "All right," he said.

"All right," Jay said. "Why didn't you stay with it? Why did you let it go?"

Peter thought a moment. "Jay," he said. "It's not complicated."

Jay waited.

"I didn't love her," Peter said.

"Yes. Okay. I knew that," Jay said. "I'm sure I knew that. Was there something else?"

"Oh," Peter said. He leaned back in his chair, laced his fingers behind his head. "Did I see this in her? That's what you mean."

"Really, I don't know what I mean." Jay finished off the iced tea in his glass. "Did you?" he said.

"No," Peter said.

"No," Jay said. "Nor did I."

The waitress brought the check. Peter took it.

"No," Jay said.

"Easy," Peter said. "You get the next one."

The two men stood up to leave. They were facing each other across the table. "Thanks," Jay said.

"Forget it."

Jay put his hands in his pockets and bowed his head. He took a deep breath, then looked up at Peter. "She was beautiful," he said.

"She was," Peter said.

"She was, wasn't she?"

"Sure she was," Peter said.

In the late afternoon they drove back to Sparta. Peter followed Jay in his pickup, towing the trailer with two horses he was taking to Michigan. Before they left River Falls Jay called home.

"Tell your mother we're coming," he said to Eli. "Tell her Peter can stay for only a minute."

Eli was outside when they arrived. He was sitting on the front steps drinking juice from a carton and reading a book. There was a gash on his knee and a string of dried blood down the front of his leg. He stood up when Jay and Peter approached him.

"Hello, son," Peter said.

"Hello," Eli said.

"Your leg is bleeding," Jay said.

"I know," Eli said.

"What happened to it?"

"I cut it. In the bushes."

"What were you doing in the bushes?" Jay said.

"I was looking for my tennis ball."

"You get that cleaned up," Jay said.

"Here," Peter said. "Come on with me. I think we can save the leg." Peter took Eli to the truck, opened the door, and sat him sideways on the front seat. From behind the seat Peter took a first-aid kit. He soaked a cotton ball with hydrogen peroxide, dabbed Eli's knee, wiped the dried blood from his leg, then put a band-aid on the cut. "How's that, cowboy?"

"Good," Eli said.

Peter whacked him on the thigh, and Eli hopped down. "Now wait," Peter said. "I've got something for you."

Again Peter reached behind the seat. He came out with a small leather drawstring pouch. "These were mine when I was your age."

Eli opened the pouch and took out a pair of spurs. They were gal-leg roping spurs, Peter explained, so called because of their shape and the brass overlay on their shanks. They had ten-point rowels, and *Peter* in raised brass on the heel cups.

"What have you got?" Jay asked Eli.

"Spurs," Eli said. He showed them to Jay.

"Wow," Jay said to Peter. "Thank you."

"Thanks," Eli said.

Lucy was outside, standing on the top step. She was wearing cut-off jeans and a plain white T-shirt. Her hair was tied back. She had showered. She looked fresh. Peter saw her first. "Lucy," he said.

"Mom," Eli said. "Look." He held up the spurs. "He gave them to me."

Lucy came down the steps. Jay met her halfway up the walk.

"You okay?" he said.

"Stop," she said. She walked past him. "What are they?" she said to Eli.

"Spurs," he said. He showed them to her.

"What a great thing," she said to Peter. She raised up and kissed him. "Hello, you," she said.

"Hello," Peter said.

Lucy reached for Peter and embraced him. "I didn't want to miss you again," she said.

"I'm glad," Peter said.

She looked at herself, then gestured—a downward flick with both hands—to indicate she was disheartened by her appearance. "Sorry," she said.

"No," Peter said. "You look good."

She smiled. "That's a lie," she said.

"He's right," Jay said. "You do."

"Well, thank you both," she said. She took Peter's hands in hers. "Will you come inside? I've made some tea."

"I'd like that," Peter said.

"Do you have time?" Jay said.

"A few minutes," Peter said.

"Are you sure?" Jay said.

Lucy looked at Jay. "What is this?" she said.

"I'm sure," Peter said. "A few minutes."

"Good," Jay said. "Good. You two go."

Jay and Eli stayed out front. Jay tried to teach his son stoop ball, a game he had played in Queens. Jay threw the tennis ball against the steps so that it came back to him on a fly. Eli didn't throw the ball hard enough, or he threw it too high, and it clattered off the front door.

"Stay with it," Jay said.

"I don't want to," Eli said. He sat down on the steps to read.

Jay walked over to Peter's truck and looked in. The windows were down. The cab was cluttered with stuff: a cellular phone, a stack of maps, a small duffel open and filled with laundry, a sack of dry dog food, a sleeping bag rolled and tied, a bed pillow, several hardback books, sunglasses, gloves, a pile of newspaper, a shaving kit, a towel, a lariat, and a pair of running shoes. Attached to the dash were a compass, coffee mug, and note pad. A leather hatband hung from the rearview mirror. The dogs lay asleep on the narrow floor behind the front seat. Jay stuck his head in and clucked his tongue. The coyote looked up at him and growled.

Peter and Lucy sat on the screened porch for half an hour, then Peter came out alone. Jay saw him speak to Eli. Peter put his hand on Eli's head, they shook hands, and Eli went inside. Peter came down the walk towards his truck. He looked tired.

"Have you got to leave?" Jay said.

"I do," Peter said.

"Right away?"

"Yes."

"Okay," Jay said. "So. It's been good to see you."

The two men shook hands. Peter opened the door to his truck, then turned to face Jay.

"Did I do this?" Jay said.

"I don't know," Peter said.

"I don't either," Jay said. "What did she say?"

"She didn't."

"She wouldn't," Jay said. "Maybe I did."

"I don't know," Peter said. He got into the truck and started it up.

"What a mess," Jay said.

"Seems like it." Peter found his sunglasses on the seat beside him and put them on. "Go easy, Jay."

Jay wanted to see Peter's eyes. "I will."

"Watch yourself," Peter said.

Jay stepped back from the truck, and Peter pulled away.

Jay found Lucy where Peter had left her. She was sitting on the screened porch, her head resting on the back of the wicker love seat, her eyes closed, her hands folded in her lap.

Jay stood in the kitchen and looked out at her. He could tell by the redness around her eyes she had been crying, but she was quiet now.

Eli was sitting on the kitchen floor, at the entrance to the porch, his back against the doorjamb, his knees pulled to his chest. He held in each hand a spur. He was blocking the way.

"Excuse me, kiddo," Jay said. "I need to talk to your mother. Can you let me through?"

Eli looked up at Jay. He did not say a word. He did not move.

Siobhan Dowd and Jake Kreilkamp—program director and coordinator,
respectively, of PEN American Center's Freedom-to-Write Committee—write
this column regularly, alerting readers to the plight of writers around the
world who deserve our awareness and our writing action.

Silenced Voices: Irene Fernandez
by Siobhan Dowd

*J*t appears that the offence
of 'publishing false news'
is becoming a fad, with the
purpose of arresting and
charging government critics,"
said opposition Member of
Parliament Lim Kit Siang of
Malaysia recently. "At this
rate, a club could be formed
of all those who have been so
charged." Perhaps the most
prominent member of this
new "club" is the woman

Irene Fernandez

writer and human-rights activist Irene Fernandez, who faces up to three years in jail if found guilty. Her case, perhaps more than most in Malaysia's thirty-four-year history, has attracted international concern and highlighted the crossroads at which Malaysia has found itself.

Malaysia came into being in 1963, when the United Kingdom relinquished sovereignty over Singapore, North Borneo, and Sarawak. In 1965, Singapore seceded. The population is predominantly Malay and Chinese. Rapid economic growth, the story of much of Asia's business world in recent years, applies also to Malaysia. Along with Japan, Hong Kong, China, South Korea, and Singapore, Malaysia is booming. Denizens of the poorer neighbors—Indonesia, Bangladesh, the Philippines, Thailand, Burma, and Pakistan— are flocking to places such as the Malay peninsula in search of work. Migrant labor is common and the rights of these often undocumented aliens have more or less gone by the board.

In the Malaysian context, nobody has been as successful or dogged in drawing attention to the problems faced by migrant workers as Irene Fernandez. Fernandez, aged fifty, is the director of Tenaganita ("Women Force"), a women's non-governmental organization based in Kuala Lumpur, the Malaysian capital. She has long been an outspoken critic of the Prime Minister Mahathir Mohamad and his government's policy of putting economic development ahead of personal freedoms. In July 1995, in a public press conference, she announced Tenaganita's findings of severe abuses of migrant workers in immigration detention camps, information her organization came upon in a project on HIV/AIDS and migration. A report issued the following month entitled "Abuse, Torture, and Dehumanized Treatment of Migrant Workers at Detention Camps" attracted both extensive press coverage and the ire of government officials. The report described mistreatment of inmates by camp guards, including beatings and sexual assaults. It also described abysmal conditions: inadequate water and food supplies, poor toilet facilities, and inadequate medical care. It argued that the numerous deaths of inmates were due either to the physical abuse they endured or medical neglect. Most died from easily treatable conditions such as diarrhea and beri beri.

After the report appeared, one police field commander in charge of a detention camp featured in the report filed a defamation complaint against Fernandez. Extensive police interviews of Fernandez followed. She refused to identify the sources of her information, as she believed to do so would only worsen the conditions of those inmates whom she had interviewed. Other Tenaganita staff members were therefore interrogated.

In March 1996, a deadline Fernandez was given to surrender all documents connected to her report elapsed, and she was arrested under the 1984 Printing Presses and Publication Act for malicious publication of false information. She was accused on sixteen counts of inaccurate information and released on bail. The trial against her has dragged interminably on ever since, wearing down both her patience and the resources of Tenaganita. This year, the group's offices were raided by police, and soon afterwards Fernandez was additionally accused of failing to file reports of Tenaganita's annual meetings with the proper authorities. Local commentators viewed this second charge as essentially harassment, designed to impede the organization in its efforts to carry out its mission. The charges were dropped during the summer. Despite these distractions, Tenaganita's work has continued. In March 1997, for example, the group hosted a regional conference on AIDS and migration.

In an interview with the on-line Multinational Monitor last December, Fernandez explained why the abuse of migrant rights was so disturbing to her group. "Migrant workers are the most unprotected labor group in the country," she said. "The employers hold their passports. The recruiting agency promises them $300 a month, for example, but the minute they arrive in Malaysia, a new contract is substituted, for $100 in wages. Often the agency takes as much as forty percent. It is worst for women. If a migrant woman becomes pregnant, she is immediately deported. This is a totally discriminatory act. Women migrant workers, especially domestic help, are often raped, but such cases are notoriously difficult to prove." Asked to identify the multinational companies using (or rather, exploiting) such migrant labor, she mentioned Nestle, Bata, Matsushita, and the U.S. electronics companies Harris and Seagate. "We are still searching for answers," she said. "Inequalities between countries are going to sharpen, and labor is going to chase capital." Asked what her advice to migrants would be, she said, "I would like all of them to go back. Their lives would be better."

At the time of press, the trial continues, with witnesses for the prosecution giving long, detailed accounts, hinging on the minutia of camp conditions and supplying evidence such as water bills. Trial dates to hear out the prosecution have been scheduled through October, after which the defense will begin its case. Meanwhile, an independent inquiry into camp conditions did confirm the large number of deaths and the essential truthfulness of the report. Trial observers from such groups as Human Rights Watch and the International Commission of Jurists have concluded that the trial itself is yet another attempt to silence Fernandez and like-minded writers and activists. "Local NGOs [non-governmental organizations] are nervous," reports Jeannine Guthrie of Human Rights Watch. "They are watching this case carefully to determine how far they can go in their own advocacy. Some have pulled back in the meantime."

Please write letters appealing for all charges against Irene Fernandez to be dropped to:

Datuk Mohtar Abdullah
Attorney General's Chambers
Jabatan Peguam Negara Malaysia
Tingkat 20, Bangunan Bank Rakyat
Jalan Tangsi
50512 Kuala Lumpur

Patricia Page

*I still smile this way for the camera, a little hopeful,
but not too. My daughter tells me that rickrack—the zigzag
trim on the ruffle of my dress—is coming back.*

Patricia Page's novel *Hope's Cadillac* was published by W.W. Norton last year. She has had short stories published by the *New Yorker* and *American Fiction* and received an honorable mention in *The Best American Short Stories, 1985*. She was a Yaddo fellow in 1987 and 1988 and writer-in-residence at Centrum Center for the Arts in 1989.

Page lives in California on a ranch by the Pacific, where, during elephant-seal-breeding season, she goes to sleep to the odd vocalization of the males. They sound like motorcycles cranking up.

Patricia Page

PATRICIA PAGE
Solitaire

*S*ince it's New Year's Day, the visiting nurse won't be coming. That's fine; he can change his own dressing, take his own temperature. He's capable. He's conscious. At least so far as he knows.

They are called home-care nurses now, but Kenneth keeps to the older term. He likes the idea of a visit, suggesting as it does a measure of sociability and exchange, and he will miss his visit with Petunia, a young black woman, small and square, with rounded corners and a stern disposition. He likes her lack of smile. He likes challenges.

I'm a lonely little Petunia in an onion patch,
An onion patch, an onion patch,
I'm a lonely little Petunia in an onion patch,
And all I do is cry all day.

Do you know that song, Petunia?
No.
You're too young is why. You have to be old and decrepit like me to know that song. How old are you anyway, Petunia? Sweet Sixteen?
Old enough to know better, Mr. Castagnetta. You can roll down your sleeve now. Your blood pressure's fine.

My wife says I can't carry a tune in a basket, Petunia, but I don't know, I think I sound a little like Pavarotti, what do you think?
More like Donald Duck.
Oh, Petunia, cruel Petunia.

His wife Eunice is in the kitchen. Their daughter Julie will be coming for New Year's Day dinner, their only guest. I will do the cooking, she said, don't lift a finger, she said, but Eunice is already double-crossing her. Kenneth stays out of it. If he had his way, they'd skip dinner altogether. He has no appetite these days and no energy to feign enthusiasm. This may be the chief difference between Kenneth before his triple bypass and now: he has no energy to feign.

In any case, he wishes Julie had something better to do than cook New Year's Day dinner for a couple of octogenarians. This is another of Kenneth's worries. Julie needs a man, in his opinion. He wouldn't say this to her face—Julie has a short fuse, like her mother—but he thinks it, frequently. His point is not that women need men but that people need partners. You can't go it alone. It's too hard, and it's unnecessary. It's true that in marriage you have to give a little. You have to close your eyes to certain things. But it's a cold world, and everybody needs a home fire. Marriage is worth the compromises. He has always said that, although not lately.

Lately, Kenneth has been depressed, and a lot of things that used to seem securely bolted down have come loose. He attributes his sudden loss of trust and optimism to the effect of the drugs he's taking. He just doesn't feel himself. It could be worse; he could still be on morphine. He doesn't envy those drug addicts any, if what he experienced is any indication. One thing: he will never look at another French painting again for as long as he lives, which may not be all that long, so it shouldn't be such a sacrifice. Impressionist—Julie said the picture hanging on the wall of his hospital room was Impressionist, a Pissarro, she said. She described it for him; he couldn't look.

"It's very calm and peaceful, Dad, a woman in a long skirt strolling through a flower garden in front of a low, red-roofed building, white, with hollyhocks growing up along the walls. She's a little hard to make out. She sort of blends with the greenery."

The white building, that would have been the jury box. The hollyhocks must have been the jurors. Judging him, all night long, judging him with long faces, pronouncing him guilty. He wasn't guilty, but he could not make his case. Those damn drugs had him by the short hairs. He couldn't make his case, and those jurors just kept on judging, all night long, judging, there was no stopping them: guilty, guilty, guilty.

That part, of course, is over. He is home now, conscious and capable, although the incision on his chest is oozing a little, and his temperature is a bit elevated.

It takes time, Mr. Castagnetta. You'll heal. Trust your body.

Trust his body! What else has he been doing all these years? Years hauling pipe and then the so-called golden years, on his bicycle every day of his retirement, save stormy weather, which, as it turned out, didn't make a dime's worth of difference to clogged arteries. Diet, Julie says. Diet was your downfall.

He guesses he will have to learn to cook for himself. Eunice is in the kitchen right now, frying onions in a froth of butter. "I've cooked with butter and salt all my life, and I'm not going to change now," she said. "What difference can it make? You're eighty years old. Are you telling me those new arteries of yours are going to plug up in the two or three years we've got left?"

He wishes Eunice wouldn't talk like that; this penchant of hers for pinning things down wears on him. He prefers things a little more open-ended. He read in the newspaper recently that one hundred and fifteen is the official maximum life span. Not that he expects to live to be one hundred and fifteen, but just the fact that an official body of medicos thinks it's possible gives him a little ammunition for talking back.

"You're nice," that's what he used to tell Eunice her name meant. Nothing has proved further from the truth. Even back then Eunice made a point of being not nice. In fact, she has expended a lifetime of effort in being not nice.

He himself is fairly nice. He gets that impression anyway: people often say what a nice man he is. Too nice, according to Eunice. People take advantage. No one takes advantage of Eunice. He can count on her for that. When he had the plumbing business and his partner was helping himself to the petty cash, Eunice put a stop to that quick. Opposites attract.

I met my wife on New Year's Eve, Petunia, what do you think of that?

I don't think one way or another about that, Mr. Castagnetta.

Me and my pals were walking home from a party ...

Drunk.

Noooo, not all of us anyway, and not too drunk, and here she came, with her parents, no less, walking right toward us. It was, oh, one o'clock, two o'clock or so. I knew the minute I saw her I wanted to marry her. Do you believe that, Petunia?

No.

You're too young is why. You're the wrong generation. Well, you don't have to believe it. Now that you have equal rights, you can believe whatever you want. The important thing is, I believed it. And so naturally I kissed her. Right there under the streetlight. Never met her before in my life. But I kissed her and wished her a Happy New Year. And me, a shy guy. Do you believe that, Petunia?

No.

Well, it's true. Back then, it was true. Very shy.

Weeks had passed while he prowled the streets of Hanford, population eight thousand, looking for her. He was finally rewarded one day when he walked into The Record Shelf and saw her in one of those booths, listening to Sidney Bechet, one of his own personal favorites. Fate.

Eunice's family had fascinated him. They were rowdy and argumentative at table. They knew how to pound and make the dishes jump; they knew how to shout down the opposition and then hold the floor by saying everything twice. They shouted, they joked, they intimidated. People burst into tears or stormed from the table in a rage. Kenneth had been used to, first, the enforced silence of meals at the orphanage, where he had lived until he was six, and then the orderly meals of his adoptive parents, his father saying grace followed by his mother's softly anxious inquiries about the satisfactoriness of the food. Eunice's family had seemed so full of life.

Eunice could hardly wait to leave them, however, and they had moved away from Hanford as soon as they were married. She implied a poisonous past that needed escaping; she hinted at a plenitude of conditions and particulars Kenneth did not know about, and never would, his perceptual powers too blunt, his innocence too intact. She had told him one thing, though. "Defiance," she said. "Defiance kept me going."

Why don't you play you some cards, Mr. Castagnetta? It'll take your mind off things.

I don't have anyone to play with, Petunia. Except you. How about a hand of gin rummy?

I have a cancer patient next, Mr. Castagnetta. I can't be late. Do you know how to play solitaire?

Oh, sure. I'm an old hand at solitaire.

He sits at the dining-room table, laying out the cards. Julie has arrived; she and Eunice quarrel in the small space behind the breakfast bar.

Eunice is in one of her moods. When she is in one of her moods, Kenneth goes his own way, a direction mostly determined by staying out of hers. He knows her mood will pass. It will pass, and Eunice will soon be going on about some book she and her friend Minnie are reading (no sex, Minnie won't read anything about sex; at ninety-eight she doesn't have to, she says, unlike Eunice, who feels an obligation to keep up with the times and who, in any case, is not shocked—nothing can shock Eunice, he has to hand it to her). Or she will be complaining because the sweater Davy's wife Shirley has knit for her looks "biddyish." Davy's wife has a knitting machine and does a nice little business. Shirley is a smart woman, but not smart enough, evidently, to catch on to the fact that Eunice does not wear "biddyish" clothes. Eunice wears long pants that look like skirts, if she's getting dressed up, or she wears slacks and sweatshirts with shiny things on them. These are the same kind of clothes she has always worn.

He hears something slam down on the breakfast bar; he doesn't look. Breakfast bar—he never thought he'd be living in a place with a breakfast bar. He wouldn't call this place a house, although the real-estate agent had: a town house, she said, shamelessly lying through her teeth. It's an apartment is what it is. It's small and cramped and has no yard and few windows and to call it a town house is like calling the window box the north forty.

No, Kenneth does not think much of this town house, especially when he compares it to the house where he and Eunice raised their five children, or rather where Eunice raised their five children, as she would be the first to complain, Kenneth not being around much in those years, busy holding down two jobs. It was a fine house, although in poor repair, coming up on derelict actually, Kenneth's two jobs making it hard for him to be the handyman he'd never had a talent for anyway; but it was a fine house, nevertheless, built at the turn of the century, plenty of bedrooms, and an attached barn, where they'd kept two pigs, two goats, and a mob of chickens. Julie used to play Supreme Court in the hayloft. She would sit high up on a beam and swing her feet as she issued decisions to the cluster of siblings ten feet below.

"You dumb wop," Eunice had said on learning she was pregnant with their fifth and, as it happened, last child. When Eunice said wop, she must have meant Catholic, because Kenneth's name had been Stilton before it became Castagnetta, but he had entered his adoptive father's faith with all the loyalty of the rescued, a faith he had never been able to relinquish, or even cheat on. The perfection of Mary's plaster image—her flawless cheek, her faultless nose, her downcast eyes with their painted lashes—still moves him to tender obedience.

S. LEON 97-

"You should have been the mother," Julie has told him. "You're the soft-hearted one. You should have been the mother."

Maybe so. Men and women were doing that nowadays, switching around. He wouldn't have minded, if he could have skipped the diaper stage. Once past that stage, he wouldn't have minded. In fact, he regrets not seeing more of his children when they were growing up. Freeze frames, that's what the past amounts to, a stretch of long working days interspersed with freeze frames: Julie wrapped in gauzy white curtains, a moistened spit curl on each cheek; Davy hiding under the porch rather than go to mass; Tommy wobbling on his scooter; Sally hugging a kitten dressed in a doll's bonnet and nightgown; Andy sinking tin cans into the grass to make a golf course. Yes, it is with regret and alarm—did he just say alarm? He meant something else, these damn drugs were fouling up his brain—it is with regret and something else that he looks back on those days.

The quarrel in the kitchen has grown heated. Julie's two sacks of groceries sit unemptied on the breakfast bar. One of them holds a pork tenderloin, for which she has a special low-fat recipe she had planned to use. In fact, the entire meal was to be low-fat and salt-free. Julie arrived, however, to find another less suitable meal underway: a congealed Waldorf salad in the refrigerator, a ham decorated with pineapple rings and maraschino cherries in the bottom oven, and scalloped potatoes ready for the top one, needing only some milk. Julie was to have brought the milk. Eunice had asked her to bring the milk, and Julie had promised to do so. And she had. The problem was its fat content.

"You can't have scalloped potatoes with one percent," Eunice informs her bitterly. "How am I going to finish scalloped potatoes with one percent? Right here where it says, 'add milk,' I don't have any milk to add, and I *asked* you."

"Add one percent. It's that simple. Where it says, 'Add milk,' add one percent."

"It won't be scalloped potatoes."

"Yes it will. *Low-fat* scalloped potatoes. *Healthy* scalloped potatoes. *Heart-healthy* scalloped potatoes."

Their poking, pulling voices pain Kenneth. They are like wrestlers, head-to-head, hands locked on one another's shoulders, circling a pit. They can't stop struggling or they will fall in. He lays down the cards with great care and precision, one by one.

"You never do what I ask."

"I do. I always do what you ask. You said stop and pick up some milk, and I stopped and picked up some milk."

"One percent!"

"You didn't specify." I was thinking of Dad, Julie doesn't say, but Kenneth hears her anyway.

"How would you like it?" Eunice accuses. "How would you like it, one foot in the grave and can't drive to the grocery store to pick up the things you need. Can't drive because *can't see*."

Eunice is legally blind. Legally blind is not the same thing as blind: Eunice can make out shapes and can even put together a picture puzzle after turning the pieces over and over in her hand. She can write a letter, too, in a tall script requiring a page per paragraph. Driving, however, has been out of the question for five years now, constricting Eunice's universe considerably. "Housework, cooking—the things I hate I don't need eyes for. The things I *hate* I can do by heart."

Kenneth thinks about this: a heart full of hateful tasks. His own life has been easier, maybe. Or maybe not easier but less frustrating. He liked his work, more or less. At any rate, he never hated it.

Eunice should have been a fortune teller. He's serious. She has a knack for knowing what is going to happen. She gave him the shivers the time Chief Theiss and his men were searching the woods in back for the little kid that was lost, and she said, "They won't find him," and they didn't. And how many times had she said, "That brother of yours is going to call tonight," and sure enough, the phone would ring, and guess who? Eunice knew more than she said, too. Sometimes he thinks she has stored up so much more than she lets on, she has become impacted, like an aching tooth.

"We'll eat rice," Eunice says to Julie now. "I'll throw out the potatoes and fix rice. All I need for rice is *water*."

Julie's mouth purses, and she goes into the living room for her coat. She slips it on with a shrug of her shoulders and picks up her bag. The door closes behind her.

She'll always win, Kenneth wants to tell her. He places the nine of clubs beneath the ten of clubs.

When Julie returns with a quart of whole milk, Kenneth is on his third game of solitaire. He thinks he has a chance of winning this time. He needs a five of hearts. He crosses himself and thumbs one, two, three cards, flipping them over to see what the third card is. Jack of diamonds.

Eunice complains that now the ham will be done before the potatoes.

"That's okay," says Julie. "The meat will have a chance to sit and re-absorb its juices, and the potatoes will be piping hot." Her tone is crisp and authoritative, a tone reminding Kenneth of one of the nurses in the hospital. It is a dangerous tone to use with Eunice. "I'll give you 'piping hot,'" she is likely to lash out. "I'll give you 'piping hot' where you won't forget it!"

When Julie was growing up, she was afraid of Eunice. Well, they all were. Eunice had a prodigious temper. Sometimes he'd come home from work and all five kids would be on the porch. No one would be talking. It was like the five of them were hanging from strings, doing stuff, but not very convincingly. Tommy might be crouched up against the steps, fingering a miniature horse or something. Davy would be riding the railing to who knows where—out of this world, that kid. Andy, of course, would be swinging a bat or bouncing a ball off the side of the barn. Sally and Julie ... it might have been something with the girls, he thinks now, recalling Sally and Julie on the porch swing, Julie, her expression blank, Sally, looking as worried as the day she was born, which was pretty worried; even the nurse said she was born an "old soul." Julie was the oldest, Sally the youngest, and it always struck him the way Sally would have a comforting hand on Julie's, or be pushing the swing back and forth with a small sneaker while Julie's bigger ones dragged along, ankles bent.

What happened? What's going on? were questions he never asked. The way he saw it, his job was to piece everything together again in a crazy quilt of family happiness. "I'm home!" he would shout, sounding happy, happy, happy, and soon after the screen door would be unlatched, by a ghost apparently, because when he stepped into the dim laundry room, it would be empty, and Eunice would be in the kitchen, preparing dinner in a stealthy silence broken only by the sound of her knife whacking the cutting board or a lid clanging onto a pan. He often wondered at her swift passage. Did she move on invisible roller skates? Hell on wheels? He sometimes thought of her that way.

In the kitchen, he would try to distract her. He would tell stories about clever co-workers or the stupidity of supervisors. He would repeat news he had heard on the car radio on his way home. At the dinner table, the children's presence might inspire him to hold forth on the triumph of construction, his pleasure in seeing a building become itself, little by little, and his pride in being a part, a small part, but still a part of it. Yet it was remarkable how his words could be so easily drowned out on these occasions by the ting of silverware and the thud of a serving bowl set down too hard.

Julie is the only one of their children who lives close; the others are shattered across the country. Scattered, he means, scattered across the country; these damn drugs are zapping his circuits. But the kids all called him when he was in the hospital. He was getting long-distance calls every day for a while. "I have wonderful children," he told the nurses, "I have a wonderful family." They believed him. He believed himself, too, but the words weren't quite right; he felt uneasy saying them, the way he used to feel uneasy in the hand-me-down shoes he'd worn at the orphanage, which had always been a half-size too small or too large.

Strange that it was Julie who didn't move away. Of them all, Julie was Eunice's least favorite. "Julie's yours," Eunice has said to him, more than once. "Davy's mine."

At one time, Julie had wanted Eunice to get professional help. "She is sick, Dad. We must help her." This was several years ago, when Julie herself was getting professional help, frightening Kenneth, because where did he come in? He didn't ask. But he had agreed to broach the subject of professional help with Eunice.

He'd expected her to throw something at him. This happened sometimes. The very first week they were married, she had thrown a wedding present at him, a sherry glass. It had smashed against his back. He'd refused to sweep up the shards, and for days they detoured around the sparkling puddle by the door. But finally, he'd given in. Everyone does, finally.

When he mentioned professional help to her, however, she'd responded without temper. "It won't work," she'd told him. "I'm too horizontal." He is still thinking that one over.

Eunice is looking for her pot holders. "Where have you put

them?" she asks Julie.

"They're right here, Mother, by the bread box."

"I never put them by the bread box. How do you expect me to find them by the bread box? I can't *see*."

Kenneth is supposed to avoid stress. The doctor has explained to him what stress does to the heart. He gets up, goes into the bedroom, and returns with his portable CD player.

How about a little music, Mr. Castagnetta? I brought you a CD.

Dinah Shore. Dinah Shore with brown hair. How did you know, Petunia? How did you know to bring Dinah Shore with brown hair? You can't be but twenty. Dinah Shore with brown hair is way before your time. How did you know?

A little bird told me. They're reissuing all kinds of stuff on CDs now.

Petunia is kind. It is a professional kindness, and he knows that it doesn't mean he is special or anything, but it is kindness, just the same.

The oven door screeches.

"Here. Let me help you, Mother," Julie says.

"I don't want your help."

Give it up, Kenneth wants to tell Julie. He wants to save her all this effort, all this wheedling and arguing and caring and doing her duty. She cannot love, he wants to tell Julie. She cannot love. It is not her fault, but she cannot love, so give it up and find yourself a husband who can.

Kenneth puts on his earphones, presses the play button, and resumes his game of solitaire. He draws another trio of cards and turns up the four of hearts. Close.

"Kenneth! *Kenneth!*" He removes his earphones and looks up into Eunice's face, which has aged in an interesting way, he thinks. Unlike his own, a terrain of deep creases, some around his mouth, some parallel to his nose, Eunice's face is a myriad of tiny hairline cracks, like a crazed china plate, its glaze a network of very fine, crooked lines. "It's time to eat," says

Eunice. "Julie needs to set the table."

"Just a second." He reaches toward the stack of cards. He has this feeling that the next draw will bring him the five of hearts. But suddenly the cards are in the air, flying and spinning at eye level, with Eunice's hand sweeping across the table and up. He draws back as he sees her hand continuing its upward arc toward his face. He closes his eyes. He prepares for the blow, but there is no blow. Instead he receives a vision. He sees against his lids an angry red palmprint on a child's plump cheekpad, a spit curl plastered to the soft skin. His heart clenches against the force of this apparition, revelation. He wants to close his eyes, but they are already closed.

He hears Eunice return to the kitchen. The refrigerator door opens, then slams shut; jars and bottles clink and rattle. Without raising his head, Kenneth opens his eyes just a little and, through a scrim of eyelashes—this is what it might be like to be legally blind—he sees Julie standing in the kitchen looking at him, on her face the spooky look of nonoccupancy he'd seen on faces at the orphanage.

He picks up the cards—grabs them rather—with spastic, jerky movements, hands trembling. Most of them still lie on the table—some face up, some face down—but a few are on the floor, and a couple have landed on a chair. He collects them all and counts them: fifty-one. He stands up, unfolding his frame carefully, and moves slowly around the table—*go slow, Mr. Castagnetta, slow and steady, that's the name of the game here, slow and steady*—looking for the fifty-second card, and after a few minutes, he finds it, lodged in a pot of African violets on the far side of the table.

With a complete deck now, he moves to the living room, sits down on the sofa, and readjusts his earphones. His hands still shaking, he lays out the cards on the coffee table, moves the queen of diamonds beneath a king, and turns up the jack. He slips one, two, three cards from the top of the deck.

Some people play where you go through the deck one card at a time. Kenneth doesn't play that way, because then you can only go through the deck once. Whereas when you draw every third card, you can go through the deck over and over again. You always have a chance, right up to the last.

AMY HEMPEL
Writer

$\mathcal{I}$nterview
by Debra Levy and Carol Turner

Amy Hempel is the author *of* **Reasons to Live** *and* **At the Gates of the Animal Kingdom;** *she is co-editor of* **Unleashed: Poems by Writers' Dogs.** *Her new book,* **Tumble Home,** *a novella and short stories, is coming out from Scribner's this spring.*

The interview was conducted at Longmeadow House on the Bennington College campus during the January residency of

Amy Hempel

Bennington's MFA program, where Amy Hempel teaches. The interviewers are Amy's former students. The interview is frequently interrupted by the barking, scrabbling, wrestling antics of Amy's temporary "ward," Savoy, a three–month–old black Lab, and Vanessa, Jill McCorkle's two–month–old yellow Lab. From behind a door down the hall also come the frantic yelps of Keeper, Tree Swenson's five–month–old cairn terrier.

LEVY/TURNER: *We've heard you refer to* Tumble Home, *the novella in your new book, as "the long thing." There's a certain intimate horror inherent in that description. What's that about?*

HEMPEL: I had no intention or desire to write a novel, but

Glimmer Train Stories, Issue 25, Winter 1998
© *1997 Debra Levy and Carol Turner*

I did have fear of novels. I couldn't bring myself to say the word. It seemed like an impossible thing to do, even a novella. It was too overwhelming, I couldn't manage it, so I just tried to kind of come in sideways, you know, not look at it head-on. And so it became "the long thing."

Do you mean overwhelming time-wise or psyche-wise?

No, just size-wise. I write very short stories, and I couldn't imagine how to sustain something beyond fifteen manuscript pages. That was the longest thing I'd written until the novella.

Yet you seem to have found your way. There are a lot of short-short pieces that are woven together.

Well, I'm certainly not the only one to do this, but I think the only way I could conceive of doing something as long as a novella was by breaking it down into manageable portions. Some people would view a novel as breaking down into chapters; even that is too large for me to handle. Because I wrote in these little moments, or vignettes—not in a specific linear form—it made sense to me to just collect moments. It was the unit of construction for me—the vignette. Some of the vignettes are one line long; some of them are a couple of pages. It's like building a mosaic, or patching together a crazy quilt. Eventually you just trust that these stories are occurring to you for a reason, that they will ultimately cohere and be more than the parts.

Why do you think you see things in terms of moments, instead of the longer view?

I think I know why that is—it's because I don't assume I'm here for a long time. I don't assume that any of us have a long time. I think that's presumptuous, and I know exactly when I started thinking this way. It was when I was nineteen and had a serious accident and my life was imperiled for a time—a short time, but still it was, and it really spun me around. Long after I recovered, I no longer took for granted that I had all the time in the world. I would not sit down and think, Well, for the next five years, this is what I hope to be doing. I'm thinking, Well for the next five minutes, what can I think of, what comes to mind?

We've read Tumble Home, *and we've talked about it, and we don't know who the painter is that the narrator is writing to, and why she is writing to him specifically.*

It's an epistolary novella, comprised of a single letter. The narrator is writing to the painter, and you're right, the painter is never named. It doesn't really matter, in a way. I shied away from naming him because I have a horror of the "made-up" thing. The writer Sam Michel has a devastating phrase—when his own work isn't going well, he says, "It's just another made-up thing." And to me, very often, even the name of a character strikes me as a made-up thing. It is a made-up thing. I didn't want a made-up thing in the middle of this long narrative. I rarely name anything. And, it doesn't really matter, I don't think, if you come to learn that it's somebody she's met exactly once. The letter, therefore, is inappropriate in its length and revelation and seductiveness ... attempted seductiveness.

Why did you choose the epistolary form?

When I stall doing the things I'm supposed to be doing, I stall by writing letters. I write at least a dozen letters a day. I hate the telephone. I used to keep a journal—maybe this has taken its place. It comes naturally. In this program that we're all involved in at Bennington, the format is writing to each other.

Like most fiction, there are elements in the novella that are presumably autobiographical and other elements that are fiction. But would you say that the narrator's overall vision of life and the world is representative of yours?

I would say it was mine. It used to be mine. Definitely not now. I mean, the idea of focusing one's full attention in an inappropriate way on the wrong person ... I would say that was characteristic of some of my earlier years. There's an obsessional quality to the piece.

There's a sense of a close, safe circle of friends and the menacing world out there (the trees with crutches, the cemeteries), but there is this safety, and especially the safety and comfort that comes with animals.

And yet the people are nuts. It's a nuthouse! I don't know, safety is where you find it. It interests me that what you think is going to be your home, or what you think is going to be a safe place, often is not, and what you wouldn't expect to comfort you, does. Actually, at the time I started the novella (and all the stories in this book), my husband and I bought a house, and were making a home. It interested me that it was not what I imagined it would be. Perfect in ways, and yet ...

When did you start the novella?

The whole book, I probably started six years ago. The novella, I don't remember when I started. I do remember more than a two-year block, or as my former editor, Gordon Lish, calls it, a "writer's *search*," which is a much more hopeful term, I think. I had too much [material] to comfortably toss, but I was stalled for a long time. It was a very difficult time. And what was missing, it turned out, was the shape of it—that it was a letter. And a seduction. To my mind, that's equally as important as the fact that it's a letter. It is an attempt at seduction, albeit a clumsy one that can only fail. There's no way in the world that the woman writing this letter is going to capture the interest of this painter. Should he even read the entire letter, he would flee.

The narrator is extremely vulnerable—much more so than in your previous work. What prompted you to move into this territory?

Hmm. I should know this, shouldn't I? Okay, one way to answer that is, it wasn't my decision. I mean, people's vulnerabilities are interesting, but I didn't set out to look at that. I started with the place. Place has always been the most—well maybe the most—crucial thing in my work.

What prompted you to write something long instead of short?

The first few sentences. I wrote the first few sentences of

what I thought was another story, and I could tell immediately that it didn't sound like a story. The pacing early on seemed different. When I say the first few lines, I don't mean the first few lines as it appears. Originally, it began, "The trees are all on crutches." With the place. Up through the line about, "The birds are fat on seeds that did not flower. Seed packets mark our places in books." Also, "No one started here first," and, "What got me here was a six." It seemed longer, it seemed bigger.

Does your work always begin with the first sentence?

I always know the first line and the last line when I start. Even the novella, I knew the last line. I don't know what that means, but it's there.

Do you see yourself moving in this new direction, meaning longer works, or was it a temporary deviation, or do you have no idea?

I don't have any idea, because I feel like I've put everything I know, everything I've been thinking of, into the book. I feel emptied out—in a good way. I don't have a thought in my head about what's next, fiction-wise. So, as before, I'll do some magazine work, get out into the world, see some different things. Hopefully spark something. And Savoy's a big part of the picture in the next year. She is being raised to be a guide dog. I'm only doing basic obedience training.

You're doing very well.

Yeah, really good ... You know, obedience training, taking her to classes and monitoring her for about a year or more, and then she'll go into specialized guide-dog training for four months. And then hopefully she'll be paired with a partner. Unimaginable at this moment.

In Tumble Home, *there's a lot of superstition, or "fortune-courting," also poltergeists, ghosts, even UFOs. Do you see these as having a goodness to them, providing some kind of comfort and help against the menacing forces "out there"?*

I don't know about "good," but I certainly don't think that stuff is scary. It interests me that certain people seem to have a genuine access, or more information than most of us have access to. I go to psychics, every so often. I went to one recently—one a friend had also gone to, and my friend said, "You know, I think she doesn't so much predict the future as read your mind." I thought that was interesting to think about. It's no small feat, to be able to know, or to have a great sensitivity to what somebody's concerns are. Down to names, dates, places.

I don't think I would want to hear the bad stuff.

I gave the person free range. There were a couple of instances where she looked at me and said, "Do you want to hear this?" She gave me a chance not to hear it, but I was there to hear it.

Talking about her visit to the painter, the narrator, Brookmyer, says she should have probed him about "the difference between originality and creativity, about his feeling that confusion was caused by the lack of genuine feeling." What is the difference between originality and creativity?

These are ideas that the painter Robert Motherwell has discussed and written about. We did visit him a long time ago and talked to him about these things. I was quite young and preoccupied and didn't make the most of it, and didn't entirely understand—and yet they stayed with me. My understanding of it is that anybody can be "creative," in the sense that you can make a watercolor, or you can maybe write a poem, or play the piano—it's creative, it's expressing something. But how rare for it to be something that the world doesn't already contain. As for confusion being caused by a lack of genuine feeling, I take that to mean that if you really paid attention to intuition, you could answer all your own questions. Problems arise when you don't honor [your intuition].

In the novella, it's almost as if you observe a mind on the page. For instance, in the physical description, it's not the traditional "here's a picture of the character." I think your work has always been that way, but especially in the novella.

I have tremendous impatience and lack of interest in conventional description. It tells me absolutely nothing. Sometimes I can better describe a person by another person's reaction. In a story in my first book, I couldn't think of a way to sufficiently describe the charisma of a certain boy, so the narrator says, "I knew girls who saved his chewed gum." So you're describing through somebody else. I love what you said about the mind on a page.

I appropriated that from David Shields. To me that's interesting fiction, where the mind is kind of leaping around on the page.

As it does! The way it seems to me to work is, you think of something, and the story spawns another story spawns another story. There is a kind of leaping—but it's a logical, if non-linear, progression. And you just have faith that it will lead somewhere and add up to something.

You finished your book at Yaddo in the fall of 1995. At the time, you said you thought you'd feel elated and relieved. But in fact you were having nightmares and losing things.

Well, you know things aren't what you think they're going to be. I did expect to feel great and relieved, and I felt a great deal of anxiety. Clearly, it's two-fold. It's, Well, what now? And it's, What of this? What of this thing? Here's a reckoning, now you have to judge this thing or appraise the thing you've just spent all this time on. And what if it doesn't hold? And it took all that time and effort. So, it was an anxious time.

You once mentioned that you usually take a year off after the publication of a book.

Not intentionally, it's just worked out that way. It took about a year with the two previous books. I just didn't think of writing any fiction, nothing occurred to me, I had no ideas. I didn't mind that, I did other things, other kinds of writing. Since I finished the book at Yaddo, I've added one more story since the book was accepted. It's "The Children's Party."

What are you reading?

More than reading new work, lately, I find I've been doing more re-reading of things I like a lot to get me revved up to work. Barry Hannah once told me it took three trusted friends to tell him a poem was great before he'd read it, otherwise he stuck to the immortals. I kind of feel that way about short stories. One of the new things I'm reading is Toby Wolff's new collection, and the stories that will come out next year in Mark Richard's second collection. They're amazing.

What are you re-reading?

Some of the stories in *Jesus' Son* by Denis Johnson, the poems of Sharon Olds, Mark Richard, Noy Holland's *Orbit* [a novella].

You say you read a lot of poetry, but your style is completely different. You don't sound like anyone else writing right now. Is that a conscious effort?

Thank you. No. What I like about poetry generally is compression. Compression has always been hugely attractive, and rhythm, whether it's in a sentence or a line.

Why do some people dislike compression?

You mean they like everything spelled out. Certain critics go after you for that. I don't understand it—I really don't understand it. Because to me, I pay the readers the compliment, I mean I'm acknowledging that they're smart enough to get it. They don't need everything spelled out. They live downtown, they've seen tall buildings. So I don't understand it. Because you don't hear—or at least I haven't seen—the same complaints brought to poetry. I think that my concerns are more a poet's concerns and always have been. I don't understand why these things in a story would be criticized, whereas in a poem it's the norm, it's what you expect. But I guess some have certain expectations of what a story is—that a story can be this, but not that. I think it really has come from a more provincial sense, a restricted, limited sense of story, and what it can do.

What do you think is a "workshop story"? I keep seeing reviews where they say, "This is another collection of workshop stories."

I really don't know what that means. Because I've taught a lot of writing workshops and I see a lot of different kinds of stories. I guess when they use that, it's a pejorative term and refers to a story that has an adequate, workmanlike quality— I don't even know. Because I see such variety, and I always have. And the results are so different in revision. I don't see that there is a "workshop story."

Why do you think reviewers keep using that term?

Because it's a shortcut.

At a writer's conference recently, an author stated that there are only twenty-five good writers in the country today. Would you agree with that?

Of course not. I think that's one of those sound–bite things to say. I don't know if he really means that there are twenty-five specific names that he would give you.

My interpretation of it is that most people are just hacks and that there's the chosen few, the golden set.

I'd wonder what his criteria were. I mean, I'd rather hear someone say, "There are twenty-five writers whose work I really love."

Can you name some writers that you really love?

The trouble is you leave out half your friends and everyone's mad at you. I also think, not in terms of writers, but particular books and particular stories or a particular poem. Not just everything they've done. Well, Barry Hannah certainly. Mark [Richard]. My friends, Patricia Lear, Mary Robison. Those are my contemporaries. Then there are the ones who go without saying, like Grace Paley.

You've moved around a lot, and I'm curious about why place is so important to you.

In my piece "Four Women," [from the book *The Movie That Changed My Life*] I mention the period of time in my twenties living in San Francisco when I moved something like twenty-four times in six years or twenty-six times in four years—the punch line being: without ever leaving San Francisco. I described that behavior as a confusion of activity without action, of activity that wasn't getting anywhere. San Francisco was confusing because it was the most beautiful place I'd ever lived and there were earthquakes regularly. There was always a tremendous threat in the midst of extraordinary beauty. I found that so hard to reconcile, and I think I was trying to leave it, but I couldn't leave it. So I'd move a few blocks. In New York, you can't just up and move quite as easily. I was forced to stand still. And it's not surprising that that's when I started getting some work done, instead of just packing boxes and taking them to the next Victorian house and the next Victorian house.

Do you remember the exact time when you said, Okay, this is it, this is what I'm going to do, I'm going to write fiction?

I came to New York from California—that was a big part of it. I worked in publishing, which I thought was about writing, which it really isn't. And then I went to Bread Loaf, as an auditor. That was an acknowledgment and a step ahead. I was reading widely. That was in my late twenties. And then there was a general push, acceleration. And really, I was painting myself into a corner; I was never good at saying, "Why, this is what I'm going to do, by golly!" You know, with great gumption in doing it. I was painting myself into a corner, leaving no other options. Nothing to fall back on. So it had better work. By the time I took Gordon's [Lish] class at Columbia, I was about thirty or so, and I really believed there was nothing else I could do. I think that signing on for Gordon's class really was it. I was saying, I will try to do it. I won't punish myself if I'm unable to do it, but I will try to do it.

Do you think a writer should be in New York?

I don't see how it could hurt anybody, certainly early on.

You know, put your face in front of people and go to a million readings. As to whether it's essential, certainly not. For a lot of people I know, almost everyone I know, it's easier to write somewhere other than New York, because New York is about publishing, not writing.

Talk about Yaddo.

That was great. As a psychic predicted. I went to her, and she said, "I don't know what it is, but it's some project that you're working on. If you devote yourself to it in the month of November, you'll make a huge leap forward." Then she said, "And why am I thinking of the town of Saratoga?" Well, I had just the day before received my acceptance from Yaddo to spend the month of November there. I went there and hit the ground running and finished this book. It was pretty great, I loved it.

Does your teaching get in the way of your writing?

I haven't felt it to be in the way, but I'm not somebody who writes every day. I get a lot out of it personally, but I don't know that I get anything for my own writing. There are lots of things that sort of fuel your self worth—the way you might travel, for instance.

You work on a typewriter. Why?

I say it's because I can never find the time it takes to get yourself familiar with the new equipment, but every writer I know who works on a computer has lost huge amounts of work in it. And I like writing by hand, I like the feel of a certain kind of pen, and a certain kind of paper. I've heard of more writers lately writing that way. Carole Maso writes in a big artist's sketchbook.

Did you want to be a writer when you were a little girl?

I don't remember actually thinking, Oh, I want to be a writer. I wanted to be a veterinarian. I had charts of dogs, cross-sections of dogs, all over my walls. I worked for a veterinarian briefly, as a surgical assistant. Spaying—neutering male dogs. I would do the pre-op preparation. I wrote about this in "Nashville Gone to Ashes" in my first book. That was taken from my experience as a surgical assistant. I would be the one to comfort them as they came out of anesthesia, because they would be confused and frightened and they could hurt themselves, tear a bandage or something. This is the best job I've ever had in my life; I would hold the dog or the cat, just hold them tight as they came out of anesthesia. I mean, getting paid to hug dogs! It was pretty great.

Debra Levy's work appears in the *South Dakota Review*, *Sun Dog: The Southeast Review*, and the *Flying Island*. She lives in Indiana.

Carol Turner lives in Colorado. Her work appears in *First Intensity*, *Many Mountains Moving*, *Cottonwood Review*, *Primavera*, and other magazines.

Brian Champeau

Me and my ride. Buffalo, 1963.

Brian Champeau is a New Yorker who has lived in Ireland, the Philippines, Uruguay, and, now, Arizona. He is the 1996 recipient of the Emerging Fiction Writer Award from Treasure House Press and is currently finishing a collection of stories and a novel.

BRIAN CHAMPEAU

Riley

I was over the sink scrubbing Cream of Wheat from the breakfast bowls when I heard Riley's hiccuping laugh, the scissory breathing sound he makes when he's excited, then the screen door slam and tires spitting gravel in the drive. I dropped the dish in my hand and walked fast to the porch, in time to see Lorraine tearing away in her body-patched car. Riley was in her lap and I saw that he was extending an arm to the steering wheel, resting his hand on the horn but not pushing it, his head round as the moon.

There was nothing to do. Lorenzo had my car out in Scottsdale, hanging drywall for one of the contractors who would pay him late or disappear without paying him at all. He carries no beeper. I watched Lorraine cruise the stop sign at the end of the block and disappear down Hatcher.

I sub, K through 12, and I'm on the list in six districts, but I got no call yesterday, no automated voice giving me grade and location, telling me to push 1 to accept, 2 to decline. So when Lorenzo called I agreed to keep an eye on Riley. This helps Lorenzo a lot because it's one day he doesn't have to ask his mother, who's been sick lately. He and Riley moved in with her a week ago. It's a temporary thing until Lorraine straightens herself out, stops with the boozing and running around at all hours.

Lorenzo called me yesterday afternoon to tell me he would be late picking up Riley. He was looking for Lorraine. He called a few hours later to say he'd found her in a bar down on Van Buren, near the cheap room she'd rented when they split. She was drunk and was sleeping it off and he was going to stick around to make sure she was all right. I didn't hear from him again until this morning when he called and said he'd fallen asleep in a chair in her room, woke up early, and she was gone.

Riley and I got along fine. We had supper—fish sticks, canned corn, and apple sauce—all of which I know he likes. He's got clothes over here, stuff left behind from other visits, and I set him up on the bathroom sink for a little sponge scrub before bed, put a clean T-shirt and a fresh diaper on him. He slept in my dad's room, a little lord in the middle of that big bed, pillows stacked around him so he wouldn't roll out. He's a good sleeper and he conked out before I even turned off the bedroom light.

A thunderstorm like we get this time of year tore over us in the middle of the night. I think I woke up well into it because the thunder sounded like it was directly overhead and lightning strobed nonstop in the window. The rain was coming down, pounding on the roof like a kettle drum. I remembered I had Riley and was just swinging my feet onto the floor to go check on him when the door pushed open and his round little figure took a few steps inside. He saw me sitting up and did the little trundling half-walk, half-run that toddlers do to the side of the bed, whispered, "Uncla Don," his tongue unable yet to manage Uncle or John, and climbed up, lay on his stomach, his arms pillowing his head, and fell asleep immediately.

I've known Lorenzo since I moved to The Sunny when I was six. He lived with his mom and aunt across the street. I remember I was on my bike doing a circle in the street when he wheeled in behind me. I followed him when he decided to take off for the end of the street which led out to the mountains in the Preserve, a place I hadn't explored yet. We rode out together into the desert, the gouged trail full of rocks that rattled our bikes. Deep in the canyon, Lorenzo whooped loud then stopped for no reason and started counting the saguaros that stood on the near ridge like soldiers, black on silver sky. It got dark fast out there. There was only sand and saguaro, creosote and palo verde, and I remember thinking the whole world had become like this, empty scrub and black rock, and feeling something like relief, like I was part of this and not much else mattered, just saguaro and sky, the warm wind on me like a balm.

We went to ride out. Dusk was when the jackrabbits came out to nibble on whatever was green. One passed in front of us so fast it was like it was squeezed to life out of thin air right in front of us on the trail, a little light catching in its coat as it disappeared in the thrum of our wheels as fast as it came. Lorenzo whooped again when he saw it and bore down, bending his body forward on his bike, leaning up over the handlebars, but he might as well have been trying to run down the dark.

Lorenzo comes at lunchtime and I give him the news. I feel awful about the whole thing. I should have kept Riley in the highchair Lorenzo had brought over for him, kept him in my sight at all times, which is what you do when you're looking after a child.

"You didn't know my wife was a kidnapper," Lorenzo says, shaking his head. Then he asks to use the phone and makes a series of calls, looking expectantly at the ceiling, waiting, waiting, trying another number, waiting. He dials one last time before shrugging and hanging up, standing in the middle of the kitchen for a second, readjusting his blue-tinted, goggleish glasses, picking plaster from under his nails. "Was my mother at the window?" he asks.

"Not sure."

"I'll talk to her," he says, and walks out the back door. Five minutes later I hear a car in the drive and Lorenzo's saying through the screen door, "She knows no one in Phoenix." His voice is speculative, as though he were honing a theory.

I'm not sure what he's talking about. "Your mother?"

"Lorraine."

"Did your mother see anything?"

"She was asleep," he says.

"Is that Frankie?"

He nods. "*Frankenstein*, by Mary Shelley."

"Thought the starter was shot."

He holds up a screwdriver.

Frankenstein is the Dodge Rambler Lorenzo took from his uncle's yard up on the res back in high school. The roof was smashed in and the engine was useless, seized from lack of oil years before. Lorenzo pulled the engine and put in one he'd rebuilt. He cut off the squashed roof with a hacksaw, bolted on a rag top that never worked.

"Take a ride?" he says.

I don't say anything.

"Got clean underwear and a toothbrush?"

"Yeah."

"You never seen the land." He says this with the intonation that makes statements sound like questions, and that I remember thinking strange and like music when I went to his house when we were little and listened to his uncles sitting in lawn chairs in the backyard, talking, switching from Navajo to English, different words, same tones. They all wore glasses and parted their thick black hair on the side. Their faces were stony, in exact contrast to the woodwind up-and-down of their voices.

J. LEON 97-

Lorenzo folds his arms and flicks his head toward idling Frankie, says again, "Clean underwear and a toothbrush."

Lorenzo has stopped talking, which happens. We fly down 17 and I tip my head back and watch enormous clouds, lightning white, move like ships across the sky. Riley should be okay. Lorraine knows he's depending on her. I saw Riley a lot this past summer when Grace was around. Just before school ended for the year, I taught eighth grade for two straight weeks out at North Mountain Elementary. I met Grace in the break room. She taught kindergarten and was always walking around with a clear plastic shopping bag stacked with wash-off markers, Elmer's glue pots, finger paints, and rainbow sheaves of construction paper. She came over for coffee one Saturday morning when Riley was with me and she really fell for him, made it a regular thing to stop by on Saturday to see him. I did my part and made sure he was with me when she came. Lorenzo and Lorraine were glad for the break. The three of us stuck around the house usually or walked in the neighborhood, Riley pigeon-stepping along on his sausage legs like an injured linebacker, reaching up high to keep hold of Grace's hand. "Ostish," he'd say, "ostish," and point ahead with a curled finger, stick his tongue between his new front teeth. The Sunny has some weird zoning and there's still parcels of agriculture left from when the whole place was farmland. One of the old-timers has held onto his land, refused to sell or rezone. He's got a squash patch and broken tractors and farm machinery all over the place, and an ostrich run—a dozen of them running up and down like they were possessed, jumping straight up in the air, shaking dust from their fat, feathered skirts. It's two blocks from the house and we'd go and look through the fence. Riley was wide-eyed. He'd shake his shoulders and point with both arms whenever the birds made a move. We'd head back to the house then and if it was hot we'd set up the old rotary sprinkler in the backyard and let Riley walk through the water spouts in his Pampers and rubber pants. One time he raised his arm over his head and used his thumb and fingers to make a beak, scratched the grass and shook his shoulders just like the birds. Grace looked at me and said, "Couldn't you just gobble him up?" and smiled, shook her head in wonderment, her black ponytail switching on her back and her eyes three or four shades of blue in the daylight. I haven't seen her in nearly a month now and she hasn't returned my calls. Maybe she sees enough kids with school back in session.

We're well out of Phoenix now and we start climbing. Frankie sounds right, none of that putt-putt transmission noise that tells you you're going to be hiking to the nearest pay phone sometime in the next fifty miles. Lorenzo looks at me and nods as if I were on the side of the road and he were passing me by. He turns on the radio. There's the sign for Fire Ant, and I say, "Fire Ant," and point.

"Buffalo burger and fries," he says.

You can't see Fire Ant from the highway. It's ten miles down a clay road. My father used to take us, Lorenzo and me, to the Fire Ant Inn for buffalo burgers, which were actual buffalo, tastier and better for you than beef according to the scribbled sign in the window. My father had a paperback atlas called *Backroads of Arizona* and that was how he discovered Fire Ant. "Sedan can make it," he'd say as he negotiated the troughy, humped road in our Impala, doing a fast hand-over-hand on the steering wheel to clear a sharp turn. This was how his book indicated the roughness of a road: family car okay; sedan can make it; high-clearance vehicle recommended. My dad dismissed the first and third categories with, "Everyone's seen it," and, "There's nothing to see." He'd laugh wheezy out of the side of his mouth at this and tell me I could write that one down if I liked. When he went, he left me the house. On days I don't get the call, I sometimes find myself in the middle of the afternoon walking each of the rooms reassuring myself in minute detail—rug, picture frame, loose door knob—how very little has changed.

Lorenzo has the focus of a long-distance driver. His eyes deepen, liquefy, cover the road. He is perfectly still but for the minute movements of his hands on the steering wheel.

"We're going to Flagstaff," he says.

"I thought we were going all the way up," I say.

"Flagstaff," he says. "Tomorrow to Window Rock."

We climb into the mounded, high-desert grassland around Prescott. The scrub on the hills is copper and green. We're at forty-five hundred feet and it's chilly.

"Was Lorraine staying at the house?" I ask. I didn't understand why he and Riley moved instead of making her get out.

"It burned."

"The house? You're kidding. You didn't tell me."

He doesn't say anything, just stares ahead with his long-haul driver's eyes.

"What happened?"

"Burnt." He shrugs. "That's why I was with my mom."

This makes more sense now. Lorraine stays good for months, years at a time, until there's some fundamental breakdown in the operation of their lives. When Lorenzo lost the job he'd had for three years with Utne Homes, she took off without notice. He stayed up half the night waiting for her, finally gave up, went to bed. In the morning he came out to the living room and saw the trap door to the basement crawl space open, heard snoring, went over to see her asleep on the packed dirt in the tight space, an empty quart vodka bottle with a straw in it next to her sleeping head.

The last time I was in Flag was for Lorenzo and Lorraine's wedding. Most of her family didn't show because she was marrying an Indian. They had their reasons: too far, short notice, no babysitter. But she didn't buy any of it. Her father gave her away. He wore boots, new jeans, a white dress shirt, a rainbow-striped tie, and a black vest. I remember standing in my pew and looking to the back of the church for the bride, seeing Lorraine and her father come through the big wooden doors, yellow daylight streaming over their heads. Her dad was wearing a cowboy hat and he took it off as he came in, looked around quickly, then handed it to the minister standing there in his white cassock, Bible under his arm, who stared at it a second before passing it on to one of his altar boys. Lorraine wore a white dress, just below the knee. Lorenzo wore a black suit that fit him perfectly.

"We're going to see Bernard?" I ask. That's Lorraine's dad.

Lorenzo nods, takes the loop off of 17 into town.

"Did you try him on the phone?"

He shakes his head.

"He doesn't go anywhere," I say.

He shakes again.

Bernard lives up a hill on a cul-de-sac off San Francisco Street. Lorenzo and Lorraine had their wedding party in his backyard. It's gotten outright cold and Lorenzo cranks the heat. It roars from the vents but disappears in the rush of cold air coming over the windshield. He steers with his knees and puts both hands to the vent as if it were a campfire, rubs them together, shivers then hugs himself, takes back the wheel. We hit a couple of lights on old 66, cruise San Francisco with its heartland brick buildings, once seed depots and cattle auctions, now micro-breweries and mountaineering shops. We head up Bernard's steep street, go up the drive and park in back. His place is grey clapboard, three stories, high and narrow, wrap-around porch, gingerbread eaves. There's no lights on. I follow Lorenzo to the backdoor, stand there as he opens the screen, raps on the window. After a few minutes, there's shuffling and a dim light. Bernard opens the door, smiles when he sees Lorenzo, takes his hand and brings him inside, steps over to hold the screen door for me. "I watch the news in bed," he says, blinking at us, his wire-rim glasses on the end of his nose, his long, frizzy grey hair scooped behind his ears. He has a broad, sunken face and is much thinner than I remember. He points to the kitchen table, pulls out one of the chairs, moves over to the sink. I hear him clinking glasses. We sit. He sets a bottle of Black Crow and three jelly glasses on the table. Lorenzo puts his hand over one, pulls it to him.

"Right," Bernard murmurs, and pours for me then himself.

"Just missed her," Bernard says, sitting straight in his chair, flannel shirt buttoned to his neck. "I told her to wait." He sips his bourbon. "She's probably still around looking up friends and whatnot." He smiles. "The little chap is a pleasure."

"Is she drinking?" Lorenzo asks, and I see in the faint overhead light that he's flushed, his face a light purple.

"No," Bernard says. "No." We sit quietly for a minute then he says, "That's the least of it, the drinking." He puts his chin in his hand and leans his elbows on the table. "She pulls apart when she should push together. Goes way back like that." He sips bourbon then looks straight at me. "Ever seen a centrifuge at work?" He says this hotly, as though it were a point of contention between us.

Lorenzo pulls his chair closer to the table. "Yeah," he says, almost whispering.

We're quiet for a few minutes then Bernard says, "Storm windows got to go up," and sets his bourbon glass down with a solid rap on the wood table. A sliver of kitchen light is caught in his glasses and I can't make out his eyes.

"Okay," Lorenzo says, nodding certainly. "First thing." He gets up.

"Any room you like," Bernard says, waving his hand toward the entire house. "Bunk where you like."

I hear Bernard's voice as if he were talking over my shoulder. I stick my head from my sleeping bag, look around the room. There's no one. His voice is coming from the window, where I see him behind the shade wobbling on a ladder.

I get up, roll my bag, put on my boots, and find the bathroom. Downstairs there's coffee and I help myself. I hear Bernard and Lorenzo at the side of the house. I go out and see Bernard at the top of a wooden extension ladder working on something with a screwdriver. Lorenzo is planted on the bottom rung looking up at his father-in-law, who seems from this distance a collection of bony right angles. I see that he's screwing in brackets around the window. The storm windows lie against the house. They're enormous plate glass in heavy wooden frames. Another ladder lies in the grass on the other side of the driveway.

Bernard makes his way slowly down the ladder. "All right," he says when he reaches the ground. The pockets of his carpenter's apron bulge with the Z-shaped brackets. "Hoist 'em, boys."

Lorenzo pulls the ladder back from the house, jumps it to the side of the window, and ratchets it up to its full extension. He goes to the other one in the grass, waits for me to lift it with him. We carry it closer to the house, lay it flat. He stands on the bottom rung, balancing like a surfer, while I go to the other end, pick it up, lift it over my head, and start walking, going hand over hand on the rungs. When it's up, we pivot it in the grass and lean it slow-mo against the house on the other side of the window. Bernard wrestles one of the windows to us and we each take a side, start climbing, third story first. We're both huffing and puffing a little and we rest at the top, leaning into the window to hold it between us. Lorenzo pulls a couple of

Phillips heads from his boot, passes one to me, says, "One, two, three," and we heave the window into place, position it right. He tightens the top left bracket, I do the bottom right. Then he goes down and I go up, and we're through. He's leaning his back against the house now, looking out over Flag. You can see the town like on a Christmas card, the snowed-in San Francisco peak way off and the forest spread everywhere, black stands of pine and the deep burnt wine colors of turning oaks and maples.

We climb down, reposition the ladders, carry another window up between us, the second and last one on the third story. It's warm in the direct sun, the house itself absorbing and giving off heat. I smell the turpentiney smell of old paint, the glue in the cracked window glaze. Lorenzo says, "One, two, three," and we make a move to position the window, but his side gives way and I nearly fall off the ladder with the full weight of the window, which slams against the house. I struggle to pin it there, using shoulders and knees to push all my weight against the frame. I watch three cracks jag like a current through the glass, top to bottom.

"Christ!"

Lorenzo is halfway down the ladder, and I see him lean back, crane his head down the driveway, take a few more rungs, jump to the ground, dropping into a neat squat to absorb his fall, then uncoiling like a cat and sprinting down the driveway. I hear a car at the bottom of the drive. I struggle with the window, get it in front of me on the ladder, rest it on the steel toes of my boots. I lean back off the ladder and see Lorraine's car half in the street, half in the driveway. It's running and she's standing behind the open driver's door, positioning it between her and Lorenzo, who I see has his arm straight out, pointing at Riley sitting in a car seat bundled up like an Eskimo and holding his bottle with two hands against his chest. Lorenzo and Lorraine argue, their words ballooning up this way, charged but indecipherable. Suddenly Lorenzo turns and runs to the passenger side. I hear his hands clonk on the hood as he makes his way over. Lorraine has left at the same time and goes behind the car, her stickish body flitting with blurry kinetic speed to meet Lorenzo at Riley's door. Lorenzo reaches for the doorhandle and I see Lorraine's elbow come up and snap at Lorenzo's chin with the full momentum of her run. She staggers him, maybe out of pure surprise more than force, and he takes a step back, clearing a path for her to complete her circle around the car, having only half-broken her stride, and to jump in behind the wheel. She slams it into reverse and roars the engine, bottoms out in the street and is gone.

I look down to the ground to see Bernard making his way up the opposite ladder, ready to help me down with the window.

She's going up to the homesite, Lorenzo's sure of it. They did a honeymoon camp trip there and she loves the place more than he does, is always pushing to go up there. Summer's the best time, he says, but they've gone in winter too, digging a fire pit, going for long hikes into the five acres for rabbits and wood. Lorenzo is a serious camper. He's got the right tent and the proper sleeping bag for any season. He knows what cooks and keeps.

The homesite is two-and-a-half hours from Flag. We go to the Stop & Shop for supplies, then head out towards 40, which is a quick cruise to the two-laner that winds northeast to the res. It's nearly full dark now.

"She burned the house," Lorenzo says out of nowhere. He's staring ahead, no glasses, frozen and focused for the long haul, oncoming headlamps lighting him in a clean-cut profile like a face on a coin.

"I kicked her out after she didn't bother coming home two nights in one week. Changed the cylinders on the doors with the extras I got in the basement. Locked the windows, turned up the air, couldn't hear a thing if I wanted to. She might have tried banging the door down that night, I don't know."

"No sign of her in the morning. Brought the baby to my mother's, went to work. Next thing I know the place is burnt and the marshal tells me arson. She put a skillet of oil on the stove and left. Poof." He hunches his shoulders over the wheel, turns to me slowly, his eyes completely off the road, and says, "She is unfit." He refreezes, refocuses, and there's wind from every direction sucking at the open car.

The homesite is way out on dirt and gravel roads, an hour from the Window Rock intersection with the inn and the swap meet and the unfinished museum. We make our way, Frankie pulling us steadily up long clay rises and patches of mud. Lorenzo stops all of a sudden, gets out, pulls keys from his pocket, and walks to the fence at the side of the road. I hear him pop a lock. He pushes open the gate, gets back in the car, and drives us in, onto the land held in treaty trust by his family for a long time.

"Fifty-eight years," he says, answering the thought in my head.

We drop into a wash, headlights flashing down the slope, follow its stony bed around a half-mile semicircle where the land flattens out in high grass and a scatter of bent juniper, the woods thick beyond. Lorenzo kills the engine but leaves the headlights on. He goes to the trunk and starts pulling equipment and lining it up in a clearing ten feet in front the car. He's got a tent which comes in a heavy-duty plastic tube, our sleeping bags, an oversized tool box which rattles with tin pans, plates, and cups, and the cooler where we stacked our food and drinks from the Stop & Shop.

We pitch the tent in the headlights. He kicks a pit in the sand and does a quick perimeter for twigs and stumps, piles and sparks them. We spread our bags outside the tent, pop a beer and a soda from the cooler, and watch the stars come out.

I hear a car before first light, tires in the wash running over the stones with a sound like giant bottles clinking together. Lorenzo is still asleep, his entire body buried in his sleeping bag. I zip open, unsnap the tent fly, and walk outside in my long underwear. I see Lorraine's car rounding out of the wash. I see her behind the wheel, her thin face long and blurred, steering with concentration around the standing water on the road. She pulls within fifteen feet of our tent and leans over to open the passenger door. She stays down like that, stretched across the seat where I can't see her for a good three minutes, the door still swung open, then she pops up and Riley toddles out, looks around lost into the grass, blinks up into the faint purple sky thinking maybe he's dreaming. She pulls away, swinging the car into reverse, then straightening it out and creeping back down the wash.

I go over to claim Riley. He bobs his head at me, does something with his mouth, not a smile exactly. I take his hand and bring him over to the fire which still burns, sending nearly invisible smoke into the sky. I squat and he stands between my bent knees. We just watch the smoke, waiting for his dad.

Paul Rawlins

The brothers grim, circa 1976.

Paul Rawlins is a Utah native and works as an editor and writer in Salt Lake City, Utah. His first collection of short stories, *No Lie Like Love*, earned the Flannery O'Connor Award for Short Fiction and was recently released by the University of Georgia Press. "Brothers I Have" is from his second, still-in-progress collection, *Lazarus Dreaming*.

PAUL RAWLINS
Brothers I Have

Life, going how it does, never straight, but circling back on itself, has brought my brothers and me together again, living in the same big house. The house belongs to Barry, my oldest, bachelor brother. He's a biologist, a famous one I've decided, from what comes in the mail, and the papers and books with his name on them in his library. When he's traveling, which he does a lot in certain seasons of the year, I have the run of the place downstairs, and I like to sit in the red leather chair in his library and read—his old science magazines, articles about primitive tribes in South America, a little history. He'd be surprised at that. Barry's kitchen floor has sparkling Mexican tile, the hallways are hardwood, the windows tall, with true divided-light panes you don't see so often anymore. It's a fine old place, with a low-ceilinged attic where I spend most of my time when Barry's not gone.

Barry took me in when the city closed Valley High. I had no seniority with the school district, having only just started on the custodial crew at Valley, after being laid off from a software company where there had been good money even for the physical plant and cafeteria staff. Considering, I should have been better prepared for this particular rainy day. I'm embarrassed still to admit to the way I spent money when it was coming regular and thick, as if they were just carving it every week off of fresh, new loaves.

When our youngest brother, Alan, came with his wife and daughter, needing a place to stay, Barry agreed to making an apartment in the basement. He installed a lock on the door at the top of the cellar stairs for their privacy, and for six days Alan and I dug down along the house's old foundation, exposing the gritty cement beneath a window Barry had decided could be turned into an outside door.

There was no way to get a backhoe through the trees and between the crumbling brick of the houses on either side, so it was dig and sweat, with Alan looking pale and shaky at first, and resting a lot, but getting better as the week went on. It was as though his muscles filled with some sort of living juice that had puddled up while he'd been idle, and I swore to Alan that the work was making him strong again. On Thursday, I got him to take his shirt off, and we went at it like a couple of fire monkeys, bodies shiny and slick under the sun, the dirt flying out of that hole steady as a clock tick.

The whole thing brought Alan down sick, leaving his wife, Roxanne, mad enough to call me an ignorant S.O.B. right to my face. I stood there in the hole Alan and I had dug, with my back to the wall I was forming up with plywood for the concrete, and took what Roxy had to say.

"You want to kill him?" she said, chewing the words between her teeth and keeping her voice down in case Alan could hear from inside. "That's what you'll do, you stupid ape." Roxy isn't a small woman to begin with. She's tall and broad shouldered, and standing up above me with her hair bristling in the sun behind her, she looked every bit like an angry mother.

I stood in the hole and let her have her say, even told her I was sorry, until she simmered down a bit—not enough to apologize, but enough to smolder instead of flame and to keep

116   *Glimmer Train Stories*

her words to herself, her teeth clamped down tight in a way
that left her whole face hard.

I don't agree with Roxy about Alan, or much of anything, but she's the one who has to bear the greater load. She's been more mother than wife to Alan for the past nine months, since a discharge accident at the chemical plant where Alan worked almost killed him, weakening his lungs to where now he has days where he has to sit up on the edge of a chair just to breathe. I've seen it, and it's nothing I like to watch, Alan gasping like a brookie on a riverbank, his eyes wide and scared, hands clenched to the seat underneath him.

There was supposed to be a settlement, but now the word is ACE Chemical is filing bankruptcy, and a few months back Alan and Roxy didn't have enough to meet the rent. It was Roxy, I think, who first brought up the idea of moving in downstairs at Barry's. We were having a Sunday dinner at my mother's little condo. Barry was out of town, and Roxy turned to Alan and said, "What about Barry's place? Couldn't we make an apartment in the basement?" She'd lost all shyness about charity. If help was offered, she'd take it, and if it wasn't, she'd ask.

While they talked, I held little Ilene, Alan and Roxy's daughter, in my lap. I had taken my keys off their ring so she could sort them by color or size, whatever she fancied. Before she added one to its pile, she would ask what it was for. If it was for someplace or something she didn't recognize, she had to know where or what it was, if it was somewhere I worked, if she could go there or see it. I hushed her a couple of times, but mostly we just kept to ourselves and I divided my listening between Roxy and Ilene, until she held up an old key with a long cylindrical shaft and a notched square on the end.

"What's this one?" she said.

"Shhh. It's an old skeleton key your grandpa used to have." I watched her eyes grow big.

"Where are the skeletons?"

"There aren't any," I said.

"Were there skeletons in Grandpa's house?"

"No," I whispered. "He chased them all away. Then he locked them out with the key. That's why I keep it," I said, hugging her up next to me. "They can't come back and bother us now."

"Did you ever see them?" she wanted to know.

"No," I said. "It was a long time ago."

Ilene nodded and put the old key in a pile of its own.

"So, if Barry says it's okay, then," Roxy was saying.

"We'll need to ask him," Alan said, rubbing at the thick skin on the side of his thumb.

"Well, I haven't got any other ideas," Roxy said, looking at Alan. Her eyes were the greatest clue to how tired she was, to how long she had been standing up for the both of them. She had become what they needed since the accident, a no-nonsense woman with no time for the whining she got from creditors and claims adjusters, the run-around from attorneys. Roxy walked where she went these days in a straight line, eyes forward, bodies left thrashing on either side in the wake.

"Barry'll go for it," I said, while Ilene was hooking the keys she had stacked on the arm of the chair back onto their ring. "It's the only thing to do." I said this last bit to Roxy, who gave me a weak smile, then turned to my mother to ask for some Tylenol and a glass of water.

Alan and Roxy waited almost four years for little Ilene. They didn't wait not trying, but nothing seemed to take. No medical explanation; it just wanted time. But I've believed ever since that it was worth the waiting, that Ilene turned out to be the sum total of all those earlier possibilities. She favors our mother more than either Roxy or Alan in looks, a dark-haired pixie with sharp lines already in her little face. I dote on her, first of all because she is—and might always be—my only niece. But she is a charmer, too. And with Roxy out working part time and Alan on the slow mend, after they moved in, two days out of three she'd come up the stairs and knock at the back door to spend part of the day with me.

We'd read books together—picture books, plant books, story books, animal books. If it was a Thursday, we looked at the globe and decided on somewhere to take a vacation. Ilene favored countries done in shades of red or purple. Barry has enough atlases, encyclopedias, maps, and such that we could take a trip to almost any country in the world. On these trips, even if we were on the hunt for polar bears in the arctic, Ilene always pretended to ride a camel. It was a leather one Barry had brought from somewhere, not quite a foot high and outfitted with a wooden saddle and a blanket with yellow tassels hanging from the corners. I got it down for her off the shelf in the library, and she was always very careful. For myself, I took the elephant, carved out of gray-green African soapstone, with one broken tusk.

I made us both lunch about two o'clock, sandwiches— bologna or tuna fish—milk, cookies. She would eat carrots if I cut them into sticks, grapes if I'd pretend she was a seal and toss them in her mouth. She helped clean up, and then we both took a nap—Ilene until she woke or her mother came upstairs to find her, me until eight or nine, when I got up for work. I have woken to find Ilene tucking me in before she went, fussing like Roxy must over her, and leaving me a kiss on my cheek, which is a wonder beyond any words I know.

Why Barry's never married is that no woman ever wanted to work that hard, to stick it out all the way through. Barry's known women, but to be with him has to be your choice. He usually won't choose to be with you. Busyness is part of it. And it used to be when he wasn't working, he was thinking. He used to switch on a lamp three and four times a night so he could sit up on the side of his bed and jot notes in the lab book he kept open on the night table. He did it when we were growing up back home, sharing a room. I don't remember ever waking to find him asleep. He was always lying with his eyes open, almost ready to get up for that notebook or having just laid it down and checking the facts and logic in his head.

When he went to college, when he was only seventeen, it was the same. He would go for two and three days at a time, come home with his clothes wrinkled and smelly, always with a book, his black hair plastered to his head in flat curls.

He went away to the West Coast for his Ph.D., and when he came back for a job as a professor, he made himself into somebody new, all at once. He went shopping for wool pants and oxford dress shirts, loafers, sports coats. He bought this house in the Avenues and brought in nothing, other than his books, that wasn't new or antique and neat and clean. He's lived that way ever since, with a lady who comes in twice a week to tidy up and a string of neighborhood boys and landscape contractors to take care of the yard. He travels, he teaches, he belongs to boards and committees, and whether he thinks anymore like he used to, or whether he's done with that now, I don't know, but he's busy and doesn't seem to be bothered by much.

I work at the university too, now, in maintenance. Barry got me the job, I'm sure. He told me about it, said why didn't I apply, and when I got there one Thursday morning, with a fresh haircut and a suit still smelling like the dry cleaners, the woman in human resources just thumbed through my application, then nodded and dropped it on the windowsill behind her desk. She said everything was fine, I could start Monday. I sat there until she asked was there something else I wanted. Right then there wasn't, so I told her thank you and no.

That's been a couple of years ago now. I've never planned on being here forever, though once I started working Barry never mentioned anything about me moving out. He's talked to me about retirement and savings, and he's asked about the one or two women I've seen on the few occasions I've seen any since I moved in, though it seems he asks more because he thinks he ought to than because he might be interested. You reach a certain age, and people don't expect your life to change much. Barry's hasn't that I know of, even with all of us descending on him like we've done.

I don't imagine people guess how much Barry and I are alike, really. Not in brains or how important we are, but we're only a year apart, and we both look like my father, me a heavier version and Barry a thin one. Brother or not, Alan couldn't have lived here on his own with Barry the way I have. They're just too different. Alan's a worrier, high-strung, more like our mother than he's like Barry or me.

I'm the bridge between the three of us now. I know Barry, and I've lived in Alan's world. First, while Barry was away all those years at college when Alan was growing up, and since, in the heavy jobs and the dead ends that seem to make up his particular luck. Alan's the one you're always going out after at night when his car breaks down. Barry, you can tell a dozen times to call you when he gets in, and he'll still take a taxi home from the airport. I'm used to that.

But Barry's getting better about making Alan a part of his routine.

"I haven't been downstairs yet. Everything all right?" he said the other night after he got in from a week away somewhere. I was just on my way to work, and I'd stopped in the doorway of his library to catch him up while he shelved things and sorted through the mail on his desk.

"Alan had a bad night on Tuesday. Coughed up a little blood." Barry looked up when I said this.

"I went with Roxy to take him in the next morning. They kept him a few hours for some tests, then sent him home. Same old thing."

"Who's his doctor?"

"Crossley's the main one."

Barry tapped on his palm with a pencil.

"How is he now?"

"He's been all right the past couple of days. Ilene's looking after him."

"How's Roxy?" he said, going back to the mail.

"About like she's been since we met her."

Barry laughed without looking up.

"You know, we ought to put another window in down there next spring," I told him. "It's kind of dark back in the bedroom."

"You think they're going to be here that long?" Barry said.

"I think they're going to need help for awhile, even after Alan's back on his feet."

Barry faced me, his hands full of papers.

"They can stay as long they want," he said. Then he went back to unpacking.

"Kind of funny," I said after awhile.

"What?"

"All of us under the same roof again."

"Kind of," Barry said.

It was September when Ilene started kindergarten, and I switched to a 4:00 AM shift. September when I saw them through the half-open window on an afternoon I was home early. Roxy, with her dress undone halfway and wilting back behind her shoulders, Barry's mouth at her collarbone, his hands where I couldn't see them. Roxy was backed against the desk, one arm propping her up from behind, the other hooked around Barry's neck. Her eyes were closed, and I heard her hand squeak as it slipped on the polished wood.

I found Alan awake downstairs, lying on the couch, open mouthed, toying with an exercise ball in his left hand.

"Where's Ilene?" I said.

"Upstairs with Roxy, I guess, if she's back from school. What's the matter?"

"I saw the jay out back again," I told him. "She's been wanting to see it."

Alan bobbed his head and settled back onto a pillow.

"I've been going to take her down to the aviary," he started.

"You feeling any better?"

"Not too good today."

"Maybe tomorrow."

"Maybe. Something's going on, isn't it?" He let a leg drop over the edge of the couch, got up on one elbow.

"I just wanted Ilene to see the jay," I said while I backed out the door. "She might be upstairs."

I took the cement steps three at a time while Alan was yelling, "How come you're home early?"

I found Ilene in the neighbor's yard, sitting alone on one end of a dark green teeter-totter, waiting for the boy who lived there to get home from school.

"Does your mama know where you are?" I said as I came up the drive.

"She's washing clothes," Ilene told me. She sat with her feet sticking straight in front of her up the incline of the board, holding on to keep her balance, her skirt spread neatly over her knees and red tights.

"Did you ask her if you could come over here to Jamen's house?" I said. I folded my arms across the skyward end of the teeter-totter, waiting for the sun on them to sink in and help stop them shaking.

"She said for me to go play."

"Does Jamen's mother know you're out here?" I asked her.

"Nobody's home," Ilene said. She waited to see what I was going to do, then said, "Make me go up."

"Put your feet down," I told her, then I pressed the board down to my waist. At the other end, Ilene squealed and tightened her grip as she rose. The teeter-totter was a long one, better than fifteen feet, and built on a swivel, so you could spin around as you rocked up and down, like a horse on a merry-go-round. There was a circular path worn into the grass from years of tromping feet pushing off and bouncing down, and I walked it slowly, dipping Ilene up and down, keeping my end between my waist and my chest and Ilene never more than two or so feet off the ground.

"Is this when your mama always washes clothes?" I said.

"I don't know," Ilene said, kicking her feet for the ground whenever she dipped, but never quite reaching it. "Higher."

"Hang on," I said and plunged the board halfway to my knees while she shrieked.

"You'll scare the neighbors," I warned her.

"Again," she pleaded. "Higher."

I floated her up again, watching her kick her feet, hearing her laugh. As I came around the circle, I saw Alan standing in the driveway.

"Daddy," Ilene yelled.

"Both hands," I warned her. She'd let go to wave, and I let her sink as quickly as I dared, imagining her falling. She grabbed for the handle with her free hand, looking at me, wide-eyed and startled.

"Sorry, hon," I said and levered her to the ground. She got off, then skipped over to Alan and reached up for his hand.

"Did you see the jay bird?" he asked.

"Where?" she said, all eyes, scanning around the yard and the rough hedges.

"He's gone, hon," I told her. "I came looking to tell you. We'll put some peanuts out and he'll be back."

"I wanted to see him," Ilene said.

"I know you did."

"Have you been being a good girl?" Alan jiggled Ilene's hand to get her attention. "Is your mama looking for you?"

"No," she said.

"Maybe we better go find her."

"The air out here will probably do you some good, Alan," I said, squinting against the sunlight. He looked back at me, suspicious, maybe hurt that I was keeping something from him, but nothing that was going to last.

"You better take your daddy home," I said to Ilene. I was still hanging onto the high end of the teeter-totter. Alan turned with her to go, but Ilene stood and held out her other hand to me.

"Come on," she said.

Blame is not something I am parceling out. Not for Roxy. Maybe she thought she owed Barry something. More likely she thought Alan owed something to her, or somebody did, or she was just lonely. Mostly, you get what you need in life, sometimes without thinking how you're going to pay for it.

With Barry, it's different. I don't know what he might see in Roxy, except that she's at hand, and maybe she offered. But he could have gone someplace else, anywhere. Anyone.

There's a story in the Bible about a woman who married seven brothers, one after the other, as each one died. I don't like to think that way about Alan, but maybe Roxy's got her excuses. Barry, though. Barry has done the worst possible thing.

When I got to the edge of the driveway, I shook Alan by the scruff of the neck before I took little Ilene's hand. His hair was long and scraggly from not being cut, damp from sleeping all morning on the couch in the sun that shone in the doorway. His shoulder, when I let my hand drop on it, felt thin and bony, not what he was going to need to bear the weight of his own world.

126   *Glimmer Train Stories*

Julia Alvarez
Writer

Interview

by Mike Chasar and Constance Pierce

*Julia Alvarez was born in New York and spent her childhood in the Dominican Republic. Her work includes poetry (*Homecoming, Grove Press, 1984; The Other Side/El Otro Lado, *Dutton, 1985), and three novels published by Algonquin Books of Chapel Hill:* How the García Girls Lost Their Accents, *1991;* In the Time of the Butterflies, *1994; and most recently,* ¡YO! *She teaches at Middlebury College in Vermont.*

Julia Alvarez

CHASAR/PIERCE: *I'm surprised to find you pronounce 'Julia' with a hard 'J.'*

ALVAREZ: I'm so used to being a migrant, I just pick up and say my name however people say it. Maybe you called me 'Julia' [*with a hard 'J'*] so I answered to that? 'Julia' [*with a Spanish 'J'*] is my real name, and that makes me feel more like I'm touching bottom, what my name sounds like. But imagine, when I taught in Hazard, Kentucky, if I'd insisted on 'Julia' [*with a Spanish 'J'*], I'd get no takers for my poetry workshop. So no, I don't insist, and I pick up the sound of my name wherever I am and how they pronounce it or mispronounce it.

Leslie Bow, in an essay ["'For Every Gesture of Loyalty, There Doesn't Have to Be a Betrayal': Asian-American Criticism and the Politics of Locality"], discusses questions of cultural allegiance, particularly in terms of feminism, where feminism is not only interpreted as an affront to Asian patriarchy, but also as one of the faces of Western imperialism—because feminism is viewed as an export of the West. Do you encounter tensions of this sort in writing about the Dominicans? How would you respond to such an accusation of divided loyalties?

First off, let's back up and talk about Leslie Bow. If she is an Asian woman, already, by being a writer, she is transgressing. My favorite memoir, the one that freed me to write about what I know, was not by a Latino writer but an Asian-American woman, Maxine Hong Kingston. And her book starts out, "'You must not tell anyone,' my mother said, 'what I am about to tell you.'" From the very beginning she sets out that just by writing she's already overturning her whole cultural programming, betraying her culture. Being a woman, especially a woman of a minority culture where you're trained to have no public voice, that everything is *entre la familia*—already, by being a writer, you are transgressing that cultural norm. And maybe not among the intellectuals, say, in the Dominican Republic, but certainly among my family.

My mother's commentary about *The García Girls* is, "*Como las gringas*"—"Just like the *gringas*. They get on the late-night TV and they tell their secrets to all of America." When you write out of what you know, even if it's not autobiography but it's based on what you know, it's considered a betrayal of keeping it *entre la familia*. So there's that. My writing in English is also a betrayal of my being a Dominican writer, who should write in Spanish, so already I get it that way, too.

All the prescriptions are to shut up.

Yes. *The García Girls* ends, "wailing over some violation that lies at the center of my art." People always ask me, what does it mean? I'm not 100% sure, but the more I think about it, the violation is already extant in being a writer, a woman, in English, going against the grain of what she was taught, violating her tradition. But see, I'm no longer a "Dominican writer." I'm a ... hybrid person. I'm a combination person, which is what multicultural means, this combination of different influences making me up. Especially since I'm first generation, I'm aware of it because none of it has yet been made into a weave that somehow seems whole. It seems to clash. I'm so aware that I am that hybrid. I'm a woman who has to wear her *asabache* pinned on her bra but at the same time she's writing novels. But all these things make sense to me, the ways that I am a mix of this and that.

If anything, writing in English gave me a certain amount of protection, because a lot of people didn't know what I was saying. It's like Sandra Cisneros talks about, that her father can't read her books because he doesn't read English. And that gives her a kind of space in which to say things that maybe, if she felt that he were right there listening to that language, she might not say. So that helped—until they were all translated into Spanish!

At the beginning of Homecoming *you quote Czeslaw Milosz: "Language is the only homeland." How does this notion fit in with what you're saying now about English and Spanish as perhaps different homelands?*

Because language *is* the homeland. I think of a culture or language as a way of making meaning of things, creating a world in which you can live. And when you're a writer—especially when you're a writer, but I think for all of us—the house or homeland of language is where you live. So that's my first loyalty, to build that house.

Twice in Homecoming *and again in* The Other Side *you refer to the Tower of Babel. Does the story of Babel scare you?*

It scares me because to be without language is terrifying, to be unable to say what you mean. The most traumatic thing that happened to me when we came to this country, even though I knew classroom English, was that Americans opened their mouths and said things to me and I didn't know what they were saying. And I couldn't explain myself to them. It's the Cassandra complex, too—you open your mouth and you say something and people think you're mad or that you don't make sense, and to me that's very frightening. And I think that's what a poet is always fighting for, to speak a language that others can understand about the world. If someone reads your book and closes it, and it's gibberish to them or they're not enjoying it, it's the same phenomenon to me. So the Tower of Babel is, I think, every immigrant's nightmare.

I wrote a poem about this migrant worker in California who was put in a mental institution for two years because ... he actually didn't speak Spanish, but he spoke a native Indian language from Mexico, and they just thought he was ... a "paranoid schizophrenic" was the diagnosis. He didn't speak Spanish, and he was making these weird sounds, guttural sounds, so they put him in a mental institution for two years, because he couldn't tell them he wasn't mad. They caught him in a laundromat washing his clothes, with no clothes but his underwear on, and in this poem I sort of imagine why he's doing that—he was probably the only one in the place, so he was laundering everything all together. But he couldn't tell them that's what he was doing, so he was hauled off. To me, that's a terrifying story.

Could I extend it to writing? Often we work very hard on what we write so that someone will understand it the way we understand it. And yet it seems we're often misunderstood. Do you have a fear of being misunderstood? Or is it a different kind of thing—once you're satisfied that you understand your writing, you're done with it?

I'm always surprised when my work is misread. I guess if you have enough readers, there will always be some who got what you meant, so then you start to wonder how much it has to do with that person, and that person's ability or inability to perceive something. But I've found, with even most bad reviews, that I can learn something about the writing, or what didn't work for someone. Yeah, we want to write and be understood and be loved, and when somebody says, "Well, this doesn't work," it feels like the same lack of understanding, like I'm back at the Tower of Babel.

Do you think, though, that different languages can carry meaning in different ways? And if so, would that lead to an alternative interpretation of the story of Babel—that it's actually some sort of miracle that you can say something in Spanish that you can't in English?

I think so, and I think that in Spanish I'm a different person than I am in English. I understand myself differently, and I put the world together differently. I asked Marilyn Hacker, who lives part of the year in France and who writes while she's there, "Marilyn, how do you write in English hearing French all around you?" She said she has no problem with that at all; but her friends who have a native language that they don't write in, if they go to their native land and try to write in their *adopted* language, they find it hard, because they start to be absorbed in their mother tongue—back into a world they knew before they even started to write. And I find that happens to me in the Dominican Republic with Spanish. So I think that different selves get expressed in different languages. I think that because I understand something about the rhythms of Spanish, I can hear my Latino friends' Spanish in the way they write English. And one of the interesting things for me is what the rhythm of another language does to the English language: Southern writers and their sense of a sentence versus Heartland writers or a New York City writer. I hear different rhythms in their prose.

Sandra Cisneros said a similar thing about her voice in The House on Mango Street—*that as much as people say it's a child's voice, it's also an English-informed-by-Spanish voice. Is a similar thing going on in* García Girls?

I don't even hear it, because it's like a native tongue becoming merged with my writing tongue. People who know me will say to me, "Boy, I can hear your voice in the prose, the way that you put a sentence together, the way that your voice goes up or the way that you move from one thing to another," and I'm sure that's because my Spanish is part of my rhythm in English and the way I speak. I like long sentences—once, a guy in a writers workshop asked if anybody had ever told me to write shorter sentences. I thought, well, that's probably part of my Spanish rhetoric taking off, all those Faulknerian sentences, all those embellishments and asides that don't give you time to breathe.

Many scholars and critics today seem to pay more attention to the politics of a book or poem, rather than to the rhythms of a book or poem and how rhythm itself can create meaning.

Well, you're a writer, right? You read as a writer instead of as a critic or an academician. You read for different things. Sure, if you read my books because of the content and who I'm writing about, at least in these two novels, you can talk about the politics of the ethnic group, but there's also a story. A novel talks its politics by way of a story. And that's different from talking politics so that everything gets reduced to polemics. That's what's wonderful about a story. It swallows polemics up and it's more than that. It isn't just a description or a sociology. It's something else. A story does something else.

What about a story like "Liberty," which seems to me to be allegorical and which takes politics as its subject even as it's telling the story—the American is named Mr. Victor, *and he gives the family a dog named* Liberty, *and so forth? What about a story like that, where it seems like you're trying to do something overtly political?*

Can I tell you a secret?

¿Porqué no?

That's one of my least favorite stories. I think it's flatter when you do that. Rereading that piece, I wish I had thought of different names. There's always a politic in a story, because a story has a point of view, and if you're trying to create a vision of the world and you have a certain politics, you want the world to see it that way. And certainly I would call myself a writer that has a political vision of the world. But that's not the way that I want to approach my reader, head on, because I don't think that's the way people change. I like the Scheherazade method most, where you engage someone in your characters and in a plot so that they become charged and changed by the experience of reading or listening. When you reduce an experience to polemics, then instantly it becomes easy to reject a different—and therefore disturbing—point of view.

What's nice about that story—I do like it—what's nice is that you have so much detail about whatever's going on with the family that even if the reader is alerted, maybe, to think of the political situation, everyday life is going on as well, so the political reading doesn't overwhelm us.

Well, thanks for thinking so … We're back at how readers can differ in their opinions!

The book jacket on El Otro Lado [The Other Side] *reads in part, "Long before Alvarez discovered her novelist's voice, she was producing inspired and engaging poetry that helped launch one of the most vital movements in contemporary American letters: Latina literature." I'm curious how you feel, first off, about being identified as one of this movement's "launchers," and secondly, whether you see Latina literature as an actual "movement," and what that means, too.*

What I think they mean by this is that I was first a poet and I was writing poetry along with Sandra [Cisneros] and Ana Castillo and all these people. And then about 1984 I came out with *Homecoming*, my first book, and Sandra Cisneros came out with *Mango Street*, Ana Castillo came out with *Women Are Not Roses*, and we were publishing in small magazines like *Third Woman*, we were publishing in *Calyx*, we were publishing in the *Thirteenth Moon*. There would sometimes be a Native American or Hispanic American issue and we would all be in there—writing together—but we didn't think of it as launching a movement. We had just discovered each other as writers and were excited about each other's work.

Now people say that there's this boom of Latino writers, but all these people were writing before there was a boom. It's just that when the work enters the mainstream and becomes discovered—like Columbus discovered America, right?—then publishers need to put a handle on the literature. Sometimes it feels slightly offensive because it can be so reductive of the work. You realize that some of it is also marketing—*A movement has been launched!*—but there was also something to it, of finding other Latino writers and therefore a fruition. It was like me discovering Maxine Hong Kingston—to see I could write about what I knew and write about those secrets, finding Sandra Cisneros's work and saying, "Oh, I can use Spanish and English," when before, in college, it was always circled—"You're writing in English, this word is going to throw the reader off," because it wouldn't be a common word that someone would know. And there was that support we gave each other. It's so important. It sounds silly, but sometimes unless somebody says it's okay to do that, that it can be done, you don't know it can be done, especially if you're a young writer and you're being told it can't.

I remember when I was in college a famous poet came and told the class he visited that nobody could write unless it was in the language in which they first said Mama, that there had never been a great writer—poet, is what he said, and I was a poet then—there had never been a great poet who hadn't written in the language in which he had—*he*, is what he said, which already should have told me something—the language in which he had first said Mama. And the radical self-doubt that started. I thought I had been fooling myself thinking I could be a writer in English.

Contemporary writers' inclusion of Spanish with English can seem very in-your-face. It seems aggressive sometimes. And then at other times, writers parenthetically translate the Spanish, as if to be helpful, or maybe in way of initiation. Or maybe they just want to be sure that they're understood. These seem to be very different approaches.

And sometimes that, I think, annoys me—when I feel the heavy hand of the writer. So I think it's such a balance, because you are writing in English. How do you keep a rhythm and a flow and at the same time introduce what, for us, is part of English while we're talking, our little *ay*s and *caramba*s and *asabache*s and *Hoolia*s?

I tend to think, "Get used to it," that the United States is becoming more Latinized. "Get used to this. This is America."

And at the same time you want to include the reader, so to do the right kind of balancing is important. I think it's exciting—I said in an article I wrote recently that that sense of an identity as a writer can be very helpful, too. If you can have your Black Mountain Poets, and you can have your group over in Paris, why not your Latino boom!? I love to pick up a book by a Latino just because I want to see how they put it together—not that that's the only thing that I will read, but I think it's very empowering to the other writers from different cultures to not just read *Huckleberry Finn*, and not just read *Dubliners*, but to read *The House on Mango Street*, and to read *Black Boy* by Richard Wright, or *Song of Solomon* by Toni Morrison, or *Mama Day* by Gloria Naylor, or *Mambo Kings* by

Oscar Hijuelos, and to have all these ways of putting together the world.

And of course sometimes if you can't get classified, it's as if you're not there at all, you're just left out. People who put together anthologies and that kind of thing, if they can't find a way to put a writer into a category, it can be hard on the writer, too.

I think so too, and that probably happens a lot. But see, I think that finally ... people are all worried, "Is this a flash in the pan?" and, "Is literature just becoming the domain of this or that group?" I don't worry about that stuff. I think the best work is what's going to remain, and that's what we're all writing for. What was it Jean Rhys said, "Feed the sea, feed the sea"? That's what a writer wants—to feed the great sea of the greatest things that have been written and the things that have been most meaningful. And I think the best work is going to last, and the other stuff will fall to the wayside. But the stuff that falls to the wayside can even be a way to get to where that great work is going, because these other minor works can help a writer, or create a culture that helps a writer to understand something in a way that then becomes a classic. So I don't worry about it.

When you started out writing, who did you look to before the voice of the Latina in literature was out there?

Where did I get the permission to write what I know? It was from Maxine Hong Kingston. It wasn't even from a Latina writer. It was from reading a wonderful and I think classic book by an Asian-American author, *Woman Warrior*. Something about her writing about her culture, and making sense of it, gave me permission to write about mine. I'd never had that experience. I went to school pre-women's studies, pre-multicultural studies. I just read the Great Books and they were my models. Theodore Roethke as a poet, Yeats ... well, who did we read? I have a poem in there [*El Otro Lado*] about discovering Louise Bogan's *The Blue Estuaries* in a bookstore.

She was the first female living poet I had read. So those were my models and, hey, they're not bad models to have. But what was crazy was that I was trying to sound like William Butler Yeats, and I can't sound like William Butler Yeats. I sound more like the woman in the "33" sonnets—"Who touches this poem touches a woman" [*Homecoming*]—but I thought that I had to make my voice sound another way if I wanted to be a poet, an American poet. And I thought I couldn't write about my material because I had to Americanize it, I had to translate not just language but my characters, so I would never call somebody *Tía Rosa*, I would call her Aunt Rose. And I would make the few short stories I wrote back then about American families, because I thought they had to be that, because I didn't know that something else could be done.

And maybe I would have discovered it without reading Maxine Hong Kingston, but it took a while. The same thing happened with the housekeeping poems in *Homecoming*. I had set out to write "something important"—housekeeping was not "serious material." And yet when I looked back, I was brought up to keep a house. I wasn't brought up to have a college education, so I knew all this lore—my first crafts were learning how to iron, dust, sweep, make a bed—but I thought I *couldn't* write about that. I was at Yaddo, where they had given me a residency; I was having horrible writer's block, because I was trying to sound like Yeats, "Turning and turning in the widening gyre"—this huge voice! You can't visit other studios at Yaddo during the day, and so I couldn't even go talk to the other writers, and I was just so anxious. And you know what saved me? I heard the vacuum cleaner outside my door. I discovered the maids. They were all around Yaddo, cleaning up and putting lunches outside of people's doors. And I made my way down to the kitchen where there was an old cook. She had been there for about thirty years and could tell you who was a fussy eater and what so-and-so liked. And she had one of those old cookbooks held together with a rubber band, with Christmas cards and Mother's Day cards and recipe alterations written in and stuff like that, and as she was talking, I started to read her lists ... *knead, poach, stew, whip, and stir* ...

And I thought why not? If Homer can have his catalog of ships, why not a catalog of cooking techniques or of spices? Why not all the ways to iron a shirt, and how to hang out a line of wash?—those are crafts, too. And so I started writing my housekeeping poems. For once, I trusted those non-traditional models. But I learned all about writing from the traditional models—the Great Books—I learned how a sonnet works, and how to write in structured verse. I think we read a little William Carlos Williams in school. I'm not even sure. It was a much more traditional curriculum back in those dark ages. Later, it was a process of discovering other voices—maids at Yaddo, reading Maxine Hong Kingston—and giving myself permission—in part because I saw other women and *campañeras* doing what I hadn't known could be done.

I'd like to interject a little something here. I like that piece you wrote for, I believe, the New York Times, *about catching a man with rice pudding. I thought you were brave to do that in this climate. I was wondering—certainly it was a funny piece, but I didn't know if that was all you meant for it to be, or if you were asserting it against a prohibition, a censuring of ideas like "catching a man," "the way to a man's heart," etc. What did you have in mind with that piece?*

Annie Finch teaches here, you know, and she has an anthology called *A Formal Feeling Comes*, with some of my housekeeping poems in it. Some women got onto me when I was writing about housekeeping, saying that that was regressive and anti-feminist. To hell with it! All these women that I knew grew up and made a craft of it—that was their artform—and that's a long tradition that I want to celebrate. Sure, I like having other options. I can decide that I don't really want to fold my own clothes, that I don't really just want to cook in a house for a man or a family, that I want other things. But that tradition, that lore, I think, is valuable. How to put a dress together without a pattern, how to cook this or that, how to iron, or how to hang a clothesline. For instance, Ruth, my husband's mother, was a farmwife in Nebraska with five kids and just couldn't waste a whole lot of time. So there was a way to hang a wash—or *warsh,* as she calls it—so you do the least amount of ironing and it dries quick. Just that you know all of this stuff ... Why would that be regressive? It's a tradition that came out of a certain necessity, just the same way many other traditions do. Many works of art come out of singing in our chains, like Dylan Thomas said.

Certainly in Homecoming, *and less, perhaps, in* El Otro Lado, *you use various traditional forms in your poems—in Annie's anthology, for example. Do you feel any tensions between working in these forms and claiming and cultivating your own voice at the same time?*

Well, I move back and forth. I want every room of our mother's mansion—or our father's mansion, as the Bible calls it—I want to claim them all. Why can't we women write our own sonnets and sound like ourselves and not just be in sonnets as romantic decoration? Why can't I want that? I want a sonnet to be a place where a woman can have a cup of coffee and talk to a woman friend about something. And I want the sestina to be a form in which a woman who is Latina can put in Spanish words, then English words, since words and the repetition of words is so much what a sestina is about, and to have that weaving of the two languages. I want to be able to move into all these spaces and to populate them with voices that are human and humane, that sound to me like the people whom I know. It's not like, "Throw the white men out, here we come!" Their voices can be wonderful, too. It's just that I shouldn't be trying to write like a William Butler Yeats.

Did you ever think maybe instead of writing in English, instead of writing within a context of U.S. writing, to identify yourself more with

Latin American writers outside the U.S. and writing in Spanish? Was that ever an option for you?

Remember, I came to this country pre-bilingual education. English became the language that I learned things in. I was ten—that age when you start creating a sense of yourself and your understanding of the world—and it all happened to me in English. Plus, English gave me that necessary space to pull away from a way of thinking of myself, and of being, which didn't credit my wanting to be a writer. English gave me a certain freedom, I'm sure. That was part of it. Then all my training came in English—all my training, all my reading, everything—and that's the language I learned to master. I feel like, in Spanish, I can't reach the gas pedal and I can't always work the steering wheel. I don't have that sense that I can really *fine tune* what I'm saying. It's much more what I call it: my childhood language.

Do you read many Latin American writers?

More in English—more English writers. When I wrote *In the Time of the Butterflies*, I had to read most of my materials in Spanish. But I read much slower in Spanish because I don't have the training, so it's much more of an effort for me. And at the same time García Márquez, Isabel Allende, Borges, certainly Neruda—whom I've translated into English—have been great influences. Maybe if I were smarter I could be dominant in two languages like Beckett or something, but I find that I can't.

But you do see some Latino writers in the U.S. using, say, magical realism in a way that seems similar to the way Latin American writers write it—as if to say, it's with these writers that I wish to be read. I guess you're saying it's not really a choice that you have.

But I think that what we do have in common with our *compañero* writers from Latin America is that culture. For instance, I remember discovering Gabriel García Márquez and giving the novel to my father. He just couldn't put it down, and

I told him, Papi, this is called magical realism. He said, what do you mean—this is the way we think! To the Americans, it looks like magical realism, but this is the way, if you talk to a Dominican *campesino*, the way that they understand things that can happen and the way that they describe things to you.

So is he drawing a line between this "we" and those who are not you? Suggesting different habits of mind, I guess?

What I'm saying is that these Latino writers who have come from this kind of background wear their *asabaches* on their bras for protection, but also take the SATs. That's what I find interesting. We're not the magical realists. We're not wholly in that tradition. We have *that* tradition, but we also have Raymond Carver and Grace Paley.

But when he said, "This is how we think," did you know what he meant because that's also how you think, or did you think he was describing a way of thinking that you weren't included in?

When he said that, it confirmed what was happening when I was reading—the same kind of, "Oh, yes," I had while reading Maxine Hong Kingston. I felt that, "*Ay, sí,*" when I was reading García Márquez too, but that feeling wasn't my sole understanding of the world anymore, or the only way that I put it together. But I had that same feeling that my father described, but juxtaposed to something else that had happened to me since the Dominican Republic. It's *that* mixture that describes me more accurately than "Latin American writer," or even an "American mainstream writer." It's that mish mash, too, that creates such strange and, I think, funny—that clash is painful but it's also so funny—kinds of juxtapositions.

So, finally, I see myself coming out of many traditions—and mostly I read these writers because they're my teachers. I read Tolstoy if I want to learn how to do a dinner party. I also read Gabriel García Márquez to learn how to get that panoramic sense of history in what I write. We're learning all the time from who we read, right? Just because I'm reading Latin

American writers, I wouldn't necessarily tend to identify myself with them. Which is what I was saying before about Latino writers, that sure I feel there's been an empowering movement—we can write about what we know, and there are young writers coming up that look to us for strength, and there are people reading our material that now understand our culture in a different way, and understand themselves in a different way because of what we've written—all of that stuff. But I don't just want to be a "Latina writer" who writes about being "Latina." I want to be able to write about a variety of things that have to do with whatever engages me, or whatever I need to find out more about. And so far it's happened that there are Latino themes in my work, because that's so much a part of my background and what I'm interested in and the way that I see the world.

Catholicism appears over and over in your work. Do you have a different sense of Catholicism now, having experienced it both in a Dominican sense and an American one? And how does it complicate how you position yourself relative to the United States and the Dominican Republic?

I'm very interested in Catholicism right now. I've been reading a lot about saints and stigmatics. One of my favorite books is *Mariette in Ecstasy*, by Ron Hansen. I love that book. But as for identifying myself with Catholicism—well, there are two traditions in Catholicism. One is the hierarchical church tradition that's very conservative—all the church leaders that were in cahoots with the dictators in Latin America came straight out of that tradition. And then there's the tradition that Liberation Theology has aligned itself with, which is the more mystical and Marxist tradition, the more grassroots tradition of the Guadalupe and apparitions and people having visions, and which the church, the establishment, finds very hard to accept. They find it, finally, very disruptive of the power structure of the Catholic church. To say that a little poor shepherdess can talk to the Virgin Mary and have a message for the Pope—whoa! That disrupts the whole structure. I didn't always realize there were these two traditions, and I think Latin America really emphasizes this other more mystical tradition, although the first has existed very much in alliance with the dictators and the power structures. Anyhow, this more radical Catholicism is the one I identify myself with—though, for the record, I am not a practicing Catholic, and I have problems, very grave problems, with the church's stance towards women.

It's interesting that this mystical tradition is problematic here, because I think that the United States—something that is really interesting me now—has a problem with ecstatic religions. They become identified with marginal groups in Waco, Texas, or cults, because there isn't a way for this kind of ecstatic religion to be any part of the "separation of church and state." It's as if the U.S. is afraid of that kind of religion.

Not only are these experiences individually empowering, but in church history it's characteristically women—who have been excluded from the church's hierarchical structure—who experience bodily, religious ecstasies.

According to this book I've been reading—called *The Making of Saints*, about how the Catholic church has formalized the whole canonization process and the paperwork and all the stuff deciding if you're a saint or not—the Catholic church has always been an incarnational church: the Word made flesh, statues all over, relics. The Protestant church moved away from this, but Catholicism has always been a very flesh-centered church in some ways. I didn't know this, but *altar* originally meant *the place where there is a relic*, so that churches were built around a sacred spot where there had been a martyr or saint—not just God and Jesus Christ, but this whole pantheon of people whose bodies were important and who could cure with their bones or pieces of their flesh.

And at the same time we have Augustine saying the flesh is bad.

Those *are* the two traditions. Certainly they both exist in the Latino culture. How could you even separate out, in many instances, the Catholicism? It's not even a religion. It's a culture.

Is this the difference between the García girls and their maid Chucha, who sleeps in her coffin? Is this split illustrated there?

Well, Chucha comes from a voodoo tradition, which is very, very incarnation oriented. You put spells on people, you have zombies that you bring back from the dead. It's very body oriented, so she has that side of it, too. And what we have in the Dominican Republic is a combination of Catholicism and voodoo, which is called *Santería*. That's combining those two traditions, so that you go to Saint Bernadette so she can put a spell on somebody, and you put a plate of bloody entrails in front of another saint and he'll do something with that combination. But Catholicism—there's another tradition I've certainly betrayed by being a writer.

Could you talk a little about the Dominican artist who gets off on the Madonna he eventually carves Sandi's face into in García Girls? *There seems to be an interesting dynamic between art and religion and deviance going on there.*

Well, that story in *García Girls* is, in part, a critique of the Dominican Republic I grew up in where there was such a love affair with everything European and American and a real deprecating of our own traditions. Anyhow, the sculptor was tempted to ape the foreign—you know, he had a European wife. She gave art lessons with her pinkie up in the air. She had a way of describing what art was, and she saw his "native" description as madness. When he followed the native tradition and created something outrageous and erotic and exotic, these huge statues that were what really stirred him, he's put in a padlocked shed in the back of the house. That story was my revenge on this idea when I was growing up that "real art" was European. I heard my mother's voice, hanging a reproduction

of native women by Gauguin, "What beautiful art," meanwhile blind to all the "native people" around us.

That privileging of the European and American also happens racially in the Dominican Republic: that elitism of what
is white—the Spanish part as opposed to the African part—
"good hair" versus kinky hair. The whiter the better.

*Very often, you hear a denial of racism, though. "Racism exists in
the United States, not here." I've heard this every place I've been to
in Latin America. "You're the racists, not us." Of course, various
regions of the U.S. have projected similarly onto the South.*

I think our racism is a different kind of racism. In my family,
for instance, there are very dark cousins, aunts, uncles. You
would never refuse entry to your house to someone because
he or she was dark. He or she is also your cousin or uncle or
aunt! Everybody's so interrelated. But there is an *aesthetic*
racism, though it wouldn't keep you from getting ahead. Class
is what's going to keep you from getting ahead more than
color. But then the more powerful classes tend to be the white
classes and lighter-skinned classes.

*I think what you might be suggesting is that, here, racism has been
formally institutionalized, that in the past it was written into laws, and
perhaps that wasn't the case there?*

In an upper-class neighborhood in the Dominican Republic, if there's a black or dark-skinned person who owns a huge
house, well then, he's powerful and he's rich. There just isn't
the idea that "Everyone who is black is not allowed here."
Color wouldn't keep you from moving into an upper class. It's
more likely your poverty that would stop you.

*I think more and more that's the case here, don't you? That U.S.
whites are comfortable with, say, middle-class blacks, but that our class
prejudices are fairly unmitigated.*

I think that *has* changed a lot here. But if you look at the
Dominican history books and pictures of our presidents, most
of them are mulatto, from mulatto to black. Because the

Spaniards came and, unlike the American settlers, they didn't bring families and wives to create a new England here. They came as *conquistadores* and they got involved with native women or with black women, and so they created a mulatto country. That's who we are. But within that, there have been later migrants who came in, and some of them with money, who gave some of us a lighter skin. Racism feels different there, but it's something I haven't yet figured out. Maybe I'll have to write about it ...

What are you working on now?

I have a book coming out in January—*¡YO!* it's called. It's not really a sequel, but it's about the Yolanda character in *García Girls.*

Who we should link with you, more than any of the other characters in the book?

Well, you know, all of the characters are me. Do you know what I mean? It's the same as with *The Butterflies.* Whoever I was writing about, I was that voice and that person.

But are there four girls in your family? Because even in "Liberty" you had four girls.

Yes, and of course, I would be identified with the one who's a writer. And *¡YO!* is the story of the making of a writer. It's Yolanda's story, but Yolanda's never allowed to open her mouth. It's the story of the making of a writer told to us by the people who have known her, people who have had to endure this trajectory. So we hear from her mother and father. We hear from her sisters. We hear from her teacher. We hear from her students. It's sort of a portrait-of-the-artist via the people. In a way, I was trying to answer the challenge that the writer's always the one who gets to tell the story. And there are all these unempowered people, oppressed by her disclosures, the people who don't write.

Sort of a documentary of Yo going on.

And they prove to be quite good storytellers. They just think of her as the one who knows how to tell a story. But now they all get to tell a story of her, and we get this portrait of how this woman became a writer, but not from her own point of view: "I am an artist and I am sensitive and I have suffered for it." It's from the points of view of the people who have known her, and loved her, and in some cases hated her, or suffered her creativity. We hear from a stalker who stalks her. We hear from a lover. We hear from a step-daughter. We hear from a lot of people, and while we get the story of the making of the writer, we also see how each different kind of person tells a different kind of story.

It's an interesting comment on subjectivity, because "Yo" means "I," also, and yet she never gets to speak. I like the conundrums implied in that.

At the same time, what I also wanted in the book, for each of these people who aren't artists, is to show how the telling of stories is so important in helping each one live his or her life. But also, the different characters understand stories differently, so that even the stalker understands what it is to tell a story differently from the way Yo does, and we find that out in the process of what happens and what he tells us about her. Then, too, Yo, the great promoter of storytelling now has the tables turned on her ...

Mike Chasar is completing his MA in English at Miami University in Ohio. His poems have recently appeared, or are forthcoming, in *The Southern Poetry Review, Nimrod*, and *Hellas*.

Constance Pierce teaches in the creative-writing program at Miami University. Her novel, *Hope Mills*, won the most recent Pushcart Editors' Book Award and will be available from Norton this year.

The

Last

Pages

*B*efore I could write, crawl, or speak in full sentences, I drew adventures on the backs of my father's old engineering blueprints. Drawing became my first love, and I remember watching my grandmother in the backyard handling large rolls of paper, slicing them with one of her melon knives while I sat in my mother's lap. I did this drawing when I was four, and in it are the characters Poy and Claudia that I used for the story "The Other." Poy and Claudia's attraction is simple, but I believe their shared territory to be a place of departure. I suppose at four I did not know of the Trans-Siberia, or places like Vladivostock and Harbin, but held other objects to be equally fascinating: elephants and clouds and simple houses—all the things I told my father Claudia would encounter in her journey to a strange place, which, at the time, was the moon.

BRIAN CHAMPEAU

*P*aul Bowles said he used to walk around Tangier taking a deep look at everything going on around him, the collision of stories right there before his eyes and ears, then go back to his room and write up as many of them as he could. Later he went back to the stories and linked them together to make a single piece out of all the parts. I try to do the same thing, to recognize the discontinuous continuum of story going on around us all the time. "Riley" is some of what I've seen and heard in the Southwest.

*O*ld age is not for sissies. An octogenarian friend told me this, and I recalled her words more than once while writing "Solitaire." The old often face greater challenges than the young with fewer physical resources, and the past may contain as many booby-traps as fond memories. I believe, though, that the bodies of the old still contain their young, lively selves. If we fail to recognize these contradictory, persistent selves, we do not fully connect.

This photo shows my father on the left, my mother's sister, my mother—six weeks after the birth of her first child—and her brother. I am in the baby carriage at the far right. Those are hollyhocks growing on the far left.

In my novel *Hope's Cadillac*, my protagonist tries to make the case that "photography is the art of loss. Because the moment, the moment you're looking at, has passed. It's gone."

My mother died a year and a half ago, her brother the year before.

MONICA WOOD

*T*he central image in "Ernie's Ark" originated from a tale my husband told me, about a daffy neighbor who tried to build an ark by nailing planks to trees. The tale intrigued me for years, and I was glad to finally find a use for it. I am especially fond of "Ernie's Ark," probably because I was writing a textbook at the time the story emerged, and it brought such welcome relief from a laborious project. The writing of most stories involves at least some measure of torture; this one was perfect pleasure, first word to last. I hung onto it a long time before sending it out—perhaps I was protecting Ernie from the possibility of another disappointment.

Speaking of arks, this is mine—named for my two little nieces, Kate and Anna. My husband and I are their honorary aunt and uncle—their parents are our dearest friends. That's Geoff with Anna; Dan, my husband, is next; then me with Kate and Catfish. Robin, the girls' mother, is behind the camera.

STEVEN POLANSKY

$\mathcal{C}$ity boy impersonating a hand. On "Red," a rodeo stager doing his best to make me look less green. Moments after this picture was taken, my feet came out of the stirrups and my hat fell off.

PAUL RAWLINS

When *Newsweek* mentioned something about the talk of moving operations from the infamous Area 51 to a military test range outside of Green River, they dutifully noted Green River as being the home of Ray's Tavern.

Ray's, in turn, happens to be home to one of the finest burgers in the carnivorous universe. It may help that when you find yourself in Green River, you are most likely on your way to or from somewhere. Distances are long and empty in that stretch of the West—long and empty being part of what makes them such fine distances—and by the time you pull up outside of Ray's, you're also most likely hungry. I know we always seem to be.

And if they do move Area 51, I can think of no better place for road-weary extraterrestrials to get their first taste of life on earth.

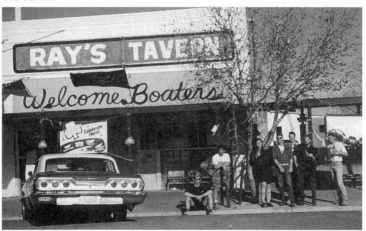

$\mathscr{P}$AST CONTRIBUTING AUTHORS AND ARTISTS
Issues 1 through 24 are available for eleven dollars each.

Robert H. Abel • Linsey Abrams • Steve Adams • Susan Alenick • Rosemary Altea • A. Manette Ansay • Margaret Atwood • Aida Baker • Brad Barkley • Kyle Ann Bates • Richard Bausch • Robert Bausch • Charles Baxter • Ann Beattie • Barbara Bechtold • Cathie Beck • Kristen Birchett • Melanie Bishop • Corinne Demas Bliss • Valerie Block • Joan Bohorfoush • Harold Brodkey • Danit Brown • Kurt McGinnis Brown • Paul Brownfield • Judy Budnitz • Evan Burton • Gerard Byrne • Jack Cady • Annie Callan • Kevin Canty • Peter Carey • Carolyn Chute • George Clark • Dennis Clemmens • Evan S. Connell • Wendy Counsil • Toi Derricotte • Tiziana di Marina • Junot Díaz • Stephen Dixon • Michael Dorris • Siobhan Dowd • Barbara Eiswerth • Mary Ellis • James English • Tony Eprile • Louise Erdrich • Zoë Evamy • Nomi Eve • Edward Falco • Michael Frank • Pete Fromm • Daniel Gabriel • Ernest Gaines • Tess Gallagher • Louis Gallo • Kent Gardien • Ellen Gilchrist • Mary Gordon • Peter Gordon • Elizabeth Graver • Paul Griner • Elizabeth Logan Harris • Marina Harris • Erin Hart • Daniel Hayes • David Haynes • Ursula Hegi • Andee Hochman • Alice Hoffman • Jack Holland • Noy Holland • Lucy Honig • Ann Hood • Linda Hornbuckle • David Huddle • Stewart David Ikeda • Lawson Fusao Inada • Elizabeth Inness-Brown • Andrea Jeyaveeran • Charles Johnson • Wayne Johnson • Thom Jones • Cyril Jones-Kellet • Elizabeth Judd • Jiri Kajanë • Hester Kaplan • Wayne Karlin • Thomas E. Kennedy • Jamaica Kincaid • Lily King • Maina wa Kinyatti • Carolyn Kizer • Jake Kreilkamp • Marilyn Krysl • Frances Kuffel • Anatoly Kurchatkin • Victoria Lancelotta • Doug Lawson • Don Lee • Jon Leon • Doris Lessing • Janice Levy • Christine Liotta • Rosina Lippi-Green • David Long • Salvatore Diego Lopez • William Luvaas • Jeff MacNelly • R. Kevin Maler • Lee Martin • Alice Mattison • Eileen McGuire • Gregory McNamee • Frank Michel • Alyce Miller • Katherine Min • Mary McGarry Morris • Bernard Mulligan • Abdelrahman Munif • Kent Nelson • Sigrid Nunez • Joyce Carol Oates • Tim O'Brien • Vana O'Brien • Mary O'Dell • Elizabeth Oness • Karen Outen • Mary Overton • Peter Parsons • Annie Proulx • Jonathan Raban • George Rabasa • Paul Rawlins • Nancy Reisman • Linda Reynolds • Anne Rice • Roxana Robinson • Stan Rogal • Frank Ronan • Elizabeth Rosen • Janice Rosenberg • Kiran Kaur Saini • Libby Schmais • Natalie Schoen • Jim Schumock • Barbara Scot • Amy Selwyn • Bob Shacochis • Evelyn Sharenov • Ami Silber • Floyd Skloot • Gregory Spatz • Lara Stapleton • Barbara Stevens • William Styron • Liz Szabla • Paul Theroux • Abigail Thomas • Randolph Thomas • Joyce Thompson • Patrick Tierney • Andrew Toos • Patricia Traxler • Christine Turner • Kathleen Tyau • Michael Upchurch • Daniel Wallace • Lance Weller • Ed Weyhing • Joan Wickersham • Lex Williford • Gary Wilson • Terry Wolverton • Monica Wood • Christopher Woods • Celia Wren • Brennan Wysong • Jane Zwinger

Coming next:

Tom reached over to the passenger seat and ran his hand along the well-worn black leather upholstery—a network of grey lines that each seemed to tell a story, like those on an old man's face. He felt very affectionate toward his car, which was, besides clothing, the only possession he had held on to through his last three marriages.

from "Angel" by Jenny Drake McPhee

Charlie was upset. He is at the stage where everything must be in order. He cannot tolerate a jacket whose zipper is not zipped up. He puts the tops back on his magic markers. He collects his pail and shovel from the sandbox before he gets out.

from "The Croup" by Gail Greiner

Now Tyler's picture of the world and his sense of mastery over it were quietly exploded. His new employer was a young company looking for contracts in overseas markets off the beaten path, and Tyler found himself going to Borneo, Chile, Saudi Arabia, and, in early 1985, Johannesburg.

from "The Cave" by Michael Upchurch

On a whim, he got out of bed and pressed a hand to his ear and jumped up and down on one foot, and then the other. But the image would not come out. He shook his head so hard that the room began to spin, and he felt nausea in his face and in his belly. When he lay back down again, shaking, he was embarrassed by his mechanical attempt at dislodging the disturbance. "But," he reasoned, "I cannot be blamed for trying."

from an interview with Nomi Eve by Linda Burmeister Davies